THE DAWN OF A
Dream

THE DAWN OF A *Dream*

THE BIG SKY COUNTRY SERIES #3

RACHEL MCBRIDE

Printed By:

Calvary PUBLISHING
FOR BAPTISTS BY BAPTISTS
CP
KJV

1902 East Cavanaugh Road • Lansing, Michigan 48910
Phone: 517.882.2112 • Fax: 517.882.2317
Web: www.calvarypublishing.org

All Scriptures are taken from the King James
Bible.

ISBN: 978-0-9788703-4-8
Library of Congress Control Number:
2007931888

Grateful acknowledgement is given to the following:

I would like to thank the Lord for His mercy, wisdom, and direction.

I thank my parents for all of their help, support, and encouragement.

I thank my sister, who is always willing to listen to my excited chatter about this book.

A big "thank you" to Brother Stauffer who took an interest in my writing and helped make this book a reality.

I also want to thank Mrs. Mercadante, Brother Wagner, and Aunt Frances Beuschel for their proofreading.

Thank you, Brother and Sister Shirey, for your support.

Thank you, Brother Ron Gearis and Rock of Ages, for printing my first book.

This book would not have been printed if it were not for all of you. Thanks!

The "Big Sky Country Series" is dedicated to the people of Fellowship Baptist Church in Cumming, Georgia, and is in memory of their pastor, Brother Randy Paul Holt.

Because of the kindness of Brother Holt and the generosity of the people of Fellowship, I was able to purchase a better computer on which to do my writing. Your sacrifice and love will never be forgotten.

Thank you!

We miss you Preacher Holt!

This book is dedicated to those who have lost a spouse.

Sam and Tom, best friends since childhood, have finally reached the Montana Territory. God grants them the desire of their hearts, and soon they have two fine ranches, the Silver Arrow and the Meadowlark.

Tony Glen has had to say goodbye to the two people he called Mom and Dad. He then meets Sam Goodton, who thinks he knows who Tony's real parents are.

After that, three unthinkable things happen; one brings joy and the other two bring sorrow. God's grace is the only thing that will sustain them and it is the only thing that will help Sam keep the promise he made many years ago.

The Dawn of a Dream

Main Characters:

Samuel Joshua Goodton: a strong Christian who longs to serve the Lord with all of his heart.

Esther Faith (Maker) Goodton: the godly, loving, caring wife of Samuel Goodton.

Matthew Joshua Goodton: the oldest son of Samuel and Esther. Matthew is the leader.

Michael Thomas and MacShane Tyler Goodton: twin sons of Samuel and Esther. Though twins, they have quite different personalities. Mike loves books while Mac loves adventure.

Montana Laramie Goodton: born prematurely, the fourth son of Samuel and Esther must be watched carefully to ensure his health.

Martin Samuel Goodton: the youngest son of Sam and Esther; a bouncy and energetic little boy.

Shane Maker: the supposedly deceased brother of Esther Maker.

Thomas Joel Sampson: Sam's eccentric yet trustworthy best friend, who is also a Christian. Together, they strive to serve God in all that they do.

Carol Joy (Grey) Sampson: Tom's sweet, Christian wife and Esther's best friend.

Special Characters:

The names Jeff and Terry Ray are taken from my Uncle Jeff McBride and his wife Terry.

The names Steven and Linda Kenneth are taken from my Uncle Steve and Aunt Linda McBride.

The names Keith and Beverly Elwood are in memory of my Dad's parents, Grandpa Keith Elwood McBride and Grandma Beverly Ann McBride.

The name Ryan Elwood is taken from my cousin Ryan McBride.

The names Jonathan and Jenny Davidson are taken from my cousin Jonathan McBride and his wife Jenny.

The name Mark Philips is taken from my cousin Mark Philip McBride.

The name Maxwell PaDave is taken from my cousin David Max Pabis II.

The names Dan and Randi Knaplen are taken from my cousin Randi Lynn Knap and her husband Dan. The name Carter Grahams is taken from their son, Carter Graham Knap.

The name Randall Holte is in memory of Pastor Randy Holt; the name Barb Holte is taken from his wife, Barbara.

The three preachers mentioned in the message on Heaven—Jake Griggs, Jack Johnson and William Kell—are in memory of preachers Jack Grigsby, John Jackson and Billy Kelly.

Chapter 1

Building

On a Tuesday morning, right after breakfast, Sam and Tom took one of their wagons and headed for Miles City. There was a lumber mill in town, The Miles City Lumber Co., and Sam and Tom had decided to buy the timber for their homes instead of cutting it themselves.

A town still seemed quite foreign to them after the months they had traveled with a wagon train. Sidewalks bustled with people and streets were filled with horses and wagons. Sam skillfully maneuvered their wagon down Main Street to Tenth Street. They had to cross a bridge over the Tongue River then pass the corral called the Diamond R. Next came the post office and telegraph office, which was in Major Borchardt's Store. Sam and Tom had already sent letters from there to tell their families that they had made it safely. Further down was the First National Bank where the two friends planned to do their banking. Not far from there was the Hotel Leighton. They also passed the blacksmith shop, the courthouse, the livery called Ringer & Johnson and finally, the lumber mill.

"Howdy, be with you in a minute." The greeting came from a man examining a stack of lumber. After jotting down a few things on a piece of paper, he addressed the two men. "My name's Jeff Ray. What can I do for you?"

"I'm Sam Goodton and this is Tom Sampson. Our families came in on the wagon train, and we're looking to build us a house. I have a sketch here of what it'll look like and how much lumber I'll need." Sam spread the sketch on a small wooden table and Mr. Ray studied it for a moment.

"I gather this isn't your first experience at building. This structure's very good. I have all the lumber you need. When do you want it?"

"As soon as possible. We might try to build two houses this year if we have time," Sam explained.

"Tell you what. You tell me where you're camped, and I'll bring it out to you Thursday morning. Will that do?"

"That'll be fine. Thank you." Sam gave him directions before he and Tom left for home.

On the way back, Tom was unusually quiet.

"What are you thinking on, partner?" Sam asked.

"I'm thinking about the goodness of God in my life. Many, many years ago our ancestors were a close family, but lost track of each other for several generations. Then your grandfather and my grandfather met—I believe by the providence of God—and became best friends. Their sons were best friends, and you and I are best friends. We grew up on the same farm and did most everything together. We even married best friends. Now we've left our home in Indiana and we're going to build, by God's grace, a ranch together." He grinned. "Isn't it amazing how God works?"

Sam nodded. "Yeah, He sure is a good God."

Wednesday night the Goodtons and Sampsons went to church, where they were pleased to see the McBrides again. They had traveled to Miles City on the same wagon train. Scott McBride had been asked to come and pastor the new church. He and his wife Cheryl and their children were living behind the church in the parsonage.

"It's good to have you and your families here," Scott said, shaking hands with Sam and Tom. "Pray for me as I preach my first message to these people."

"We will," they promised.

It was a good service. They began with prayer. Then, with Cheryl playing the piano and Brother Scott leading them, they sang a few hymns. His message was on the mercy of God.

Before the service came to a close, the pastor asked if there was anyone who would like to join the church. The Goodtons and the Sampsons were the first to do so.

Early the next morning Duke, Sam's big black dog, let out a series of deep barks, as the Goodtons and Sampsons watched several wagons loaded with lumber pull in.

"Here's your lumber," Mr. Ray said, hopping off his wagon. "Some of my men and I wondered if we could lend you folks a hand."

"That would be greatly appreciated, Mr. Ray," Sam said, after settling down his dog. "Are you sure you have time?"

"We can make time," Ray assured him. Just then another wagon, driven by a woman, pulled in.

"This is my wife Terry. She brought a wagonload of food to help feed this crowd," Jeff told them. "And believe me when I say we like to eat!"

The two families were touched. Here they were, newcomers, and yet these folks were already going out of their way to lend them a hand.

Tears welled in Sam's eyes as he expressed his thanks. "Mr. Ray, this is my wife Esther, and these are my five boys. Matthew here is the oldest. The twins are Michael and MacShane. Next to them is Montana, and the little one is Martin."

"This is my wife Carol." Tom put his arm around the golden-haired woman.

"Pleased to meet you all," the Rays said, and Jeff added, "Let's get to work."

All day the place echoed with the sounds of hammers and saws. The people from the mill, ten of them all together, were a great help. By that evening, much had been done.

"If it's okay with you, we'll be back tomorrow," Jeff said, taking a drink of cool water.

"Are you sure you folks can spare us another day?" Tom asked.

"We can. I've got two men down at the mill, and they'll let me know if I'm needed. It's been kind of slow around there anyway. Most folks are too busy with crops and cattle this time of year to think about building. Besides, we'd like to see you get your house done as soon as possible. It would be terrible if the snows came early and you were out here with no shelter. It's happened before."

"Thanks, Jeff, we can sure use the help," Sam said.

Monday morning, as Matthew handed his father some nails, he asked, "How much more time do you think it'll take, Dad?"

"Mr. Ray says it might be done by the end of this week," Sam said. He took careful aim and drove in a nail. "There, that'll hold it in place." Sam made his way down the ladder. "Where are your brothers?" he asked. Sam knew that Matt kept careful track of his younger siblings. Seldom did he not know where they were and what they were doing. That day was no exception.

"Mike and Mac are helping unload a wagon, Montana is helping Mom and Mrs. Ray, and Martin is asleep."

"Good." Sam stopped his work for a minute and studied the building in front of him. He could not believe the progress that had been made.

Duke came up with a long stick in his mouth, dropped it in front of Matthew, and wagged his tail hopefully. The boy's face beamed and, picking up the stick, he threw it with all the power of his young arm. Duke bounded after the stick and brought it back. After a few minutes of playing tug-of-war, Duke lay down at Matt's feet. Rubbing the dog's head, Matt looked at his father and then at their house.

"God's been good to us," he said.

"You're right, Warrior," Sam agreed. Each of the boys had a nickname. Matt's had been given when an Indian chief they met on the way to Miles City had told him to be a warrior for peace. Mike's was Professor, because of his love of books and learning. Mac's stocky build had earned him the name Lumberjack. Montana, who had fought to stay alive after being born pre-maturely, had been nicknamed

Soldier. Martin, on the go most of the time, was called Tornado.

By the eleventh of September, the exterior of the house was finished and a barn had been built as well.

"Thank you so much for what you have done for us," Carol said to Terry.

"You're welcome," she replied. "We all know what it's like to come to a new place without many friends. Someone lent us a hand, and we try to do the same for others."

"Jeff, thanks for all your help." Sam shook the man's hand. "We couldn't have done it without you and your men."

"Well, if you promise to continue buying lumber from me, we'll call it even," Jeff said, grinning.

"You've got yourself a deal." Tom punctuated the promise with a firm handshake. "Carol and I will spend this first winter with Sam and Esther. I'll be back sometime next spring when we begin building our house."

"We'll be looking for you. If you need anything, let us know." After Sam had paid him for the lumber and supplies, Jeff and his crew left.

When the last wagon had disappeared, Esther turned to face the family. "I think the boys ought to catch us fish for our first meal in the new house."

"Really?" Mike asked.

"Can we?" Mac added.

"Sounds good to me," Sam said. "Come on, boys. Let's go see what kind of fish we can get out of that creek."

After watching the seven fellows and the dog race down to the lake, Esther and Carol stepped into the house. Esther closed the door and turned to let her eyes sweep over the interior of the building. Even with boxes, trunks, and tools scattered around, it was lovely. To her right a window looked over the path leading to their house. Beyond the window was a corner where Sam had said they would put the piano. To the side of it, was a staircase that led to the bedrooms. The first room was Sam and Esther's. There was Matt's room, a sewing room, a room that Monty and Martin would share, and one for the twins. A window overlooking the pond was at the head of another set of stairs that led down to the living room. Beyond the steps was the study, and across the wide hall was a spare room. Between the two rooms were the backdoor and another window. To Esther's left, a wall separated the washroom, kitchen, and part of the dining room from the living room. A door in the corner of the dining room led outside.

"Carol, I'm so blessed. I have salvation, Sam, the boys, you for a friend, and this wonderful house." She laughed softly. "Who would have ever dreamed that we would marry best friends and travel out west together?"

Carol shook her head. "I surely didn't. I was afraid we would grow up, get married, and never see each other again, but the Lord worked it all out. We are both blessed, Esther."

Supper that night was a grand occasion. Though they had to sit on the floor to eat, the two families felt like kings and queens in a castle.

"I can't wait until we can get beds and sleep in our rooms," Mac said.

"Same here," Mike agreed.

"If you want, you can take your blankets up there and sleep in your rooms tonight," Sam told them.

"Great!" Matt exclaimed. "Dad, when are we going to get furniture in here for Mom?"

"Just as soon as I can find some. It would be good if I could make some of it this winter."

"Can we help?" Monty asked.

"Sure, Soldier. We'll do it together."

It was not until later that night, when everyone else was asleep, that Sam was able to ask Esther what she thought of the house.

"Sam, it's simply beautiful. I can't wait to start decorating." She moved to the center of the living room, walking quietly so she would not wake the boys or Tom and Carol. "Right here," she said, pointing to the left of the fireplace, "we need a rocking chair, and over there, with its back to the door, a long sofa, and a small one across from the fireplace. To the right of the fireplace, we'll need a straight-back chair. To the right of the door, we'll build a place to put your guns, and we'll need a table behind the rocker so you and Tom and the boys can play chess or checkers. We'll need a little table by the small sofa to put a lamp on and a longer table in front of the big sofa; that's where we'll lay the family Bible. In the kitchen, we'll have a long table so we can invite lots of people to come for suppers."

"Whoa, slow down," he teased. "Now let me see if I got this straight." He began to count the items on his fingers. "For the living room and dining room I need to get one rocking chair, two sofas—one long and one short—a straight-back chair, three tables, a gun cabinet, a long dining table, and one more thing, right?"

"No, that was all I said."

"You forgot one thing, a piano."

She smiled. "There is much that needs to be done, Sam. I honestly don't mind waiting until the more important things are taken care of."

"We'll see. I miss hearing you play." Together they walked to the window and looked up at the night sky.

"I love this place. It will be wonderful to watch our children grow up here," she said. "Wait a minute. That's it!"

"What?" he asked, surprised by her outburst.

"The name of the ranch. Actually, you named it."

"I did?"

"Yes, remember when you told me you wanted to watch our children grow up and our hair turn *silver* on this land? Psalms 127:4 says that children are like arrows. 'As arrows are in the hand of a mighty man; so are children of the youth.' Let's name this place the Silver Arrow. What do you think?"

"The Silver Arrow," he repeated. "That's perfect, Esther. I was reading my Bible this morning, and I read this verse. I've known about it, but the truth of it was really made clear. Psalms 50:10 says, 'For every beast of the forest is mine, and the cattle upon a thousand hills.' God owns the cattle on a thousand hills. Let's have that be our ranch verse."

"The Silver Arrow, whose God owns the cattle on a thousand hills," Esther said. "What a blessing to know that He can and will take care of us."

Chapter 2

Surprise for Esther

September 18 found a good part of the interior of the house finished. Sam and Tom had found most of the furniture, and Esther and Carol had finished hanging curtains and laying rugs.

"It really looks like home," Matthew said that evening. "Especially since Mom's curtains and pictures are up. It's like our home back in Indiana, only a lot bigger!"

"Mac and I like our room," Mike said. "We can see the creek real good from our window."

"Every time I see it, I want to go fishing." Mac sat down on the floor beside his twin. Duke sat between them, and they began to pet him.

"I like to watch the horses," Monty said. "I can see the corral from my window."

"I'm glad you boys like it. What about you, Tornado?" Esther asked Martin.

"I like it here!"

"Wonderful," Sam said. "Now, guess what we're going to do tomorrow."

"What?" the boys asked.

"I know it's late but, we're going to have a birthday party for you guys!"

"Hurray!" they shouted, and bombarded their parents with questions.

"What are we going to do?"

"Are we going to go riding?"

"What are we going to eat?"

"What about fishing?"

Duke, sensing the excitement, jumped up and began barking.

"Hold on a second, boys," Sam said, his eyes twinkling. "Matt, what would you like to do?"

"Go on a picnic."

"What about you, Mike, Mac?"

"A picnic!" the twins chorused.

"Monty?"

"A picnic!"

"What about you, Martin?"

"Picnic!"

"Well, I guess it's unanimous," Esther said. "Aunt Carol and I will make a basketful of treats, and we'll go on a picnic."

"You know," Tom said, "I was riding through the woods behind the house yesterday, and I found a meadow that's perfect for a picnic. What do you say, fellows?"

They agreed wholeheartedly. The next day the party took place. Since all of the boys were born in August, Sam and Esther had one birthday party for them. Because of the move, they had missed it the month before, but the boys did not mind. Even though it was late, they had a grand time. Matthew turned seven, the twins six, Montana five, and Martin four.

On Saturday, Sam decided it was time to look for a piano. His plan was to spend the day in town looking for one. The best place to start was Kenneth's General Store, owned by Steve Kenneth and his wife Linda. They had already befriended Sam, Tom, and their families.

As Sam drove his team down the trail, he began to pray. "Dear Lord, if it be Thy will, I pray that I could find a piano for Esther. Lord, she's been such a blessing to the boys and me. This would be an encouragement to her. I know it seems like a small matter, but You're interested in the little things of our lives. Thank

You, dear Lord, for being a God that cares for His own. I love You, Lord."

Sam was soon stopping his team in front of the general store.

"Hello, Mr. Kenneth."

"Good morning, Mr. Goodton. Fine day, isn't it?"

"Yes sir. I have a list of things that I need."

Steve took the list and studied it for a moment. "I have all this in stock. I'll fill this order right away. Anything else I can do for you?"

"One more thing. Do you know where I might be able to buy a piano?"

Steve scratched his head. "A piano . . . let me think . . . um . . . wait a minute." He opened a door that led to the storeroom. "Linda, Linda, can you come here a minute?"

His wife, tall with blue eyes and blonde hair, stepped into the store.

"Do you know if there's a piano for sale around here?" Steve asked.

"Hmm . . . Mrs. Harper had a piano, and I remember hearing her say that because of her bad eyesight she was having trouble playing it. She was thinking about selling it, but that's been a couple of months ago."

"Where does she live?" Sam asked.

"Turn left at the bank," Steve answered. "She and her husband live in the fourth house on the left."

"Thank you." After paying for his purchases, Sam drove his wagon to the Harper's house.

Sam mounted the steps and knocked. A stooped man with twinkling gray eyes responded.

"Are you Mr. Harper?"

"Last time I checked I was," the man replied cheerfully. "Come on in." Sam stepped in and followed him into a cozy living room. Sam was dismayed to see no piano in the room.

"Find yourself a seat and make yourself comfortable." The man lowered himself into a stuffed chair. "What can I do for you, son?"

"My name is Sam Goodton, and my family and I just moved here. A friend of mine told me you might have a piano for sale."

"Betsy, that's my wife, she's got a piano, and she was considering selling it. Come with me and I'll ask her. She's outside feeding her cats."

Sam, his heart racing, followed.

Mr. Harper opened the back door and called, "Betsy! Betsy, where are you, my dear?"

"Here I am, Oscar." On the back porch was a woman with her gray hair done up in a bun. Four tiger-colored cats rubbed at her ankles.

"This young fellow was wondering if you'd like to part with your piano," Mr. Harper said, nodding toward Sam.

"Oh, do you play, sonny?" she asked, wiping her hands on her apron.

"Just a little, ma'am. I really want it for my wife," Sam explained.

"I see. Come with me." Betsy led the way to a tiny room furnished with only a piano and a piano bench.

"She's an old one but plays real nice. My eyes aren't what they used to be, and it's hard for me to play. Still, I had half decided to keep her. Many a time I've come in here and plinked around on these ivory keys, but all it's doing now is collecting dust." The woman ran her hands lovingly over the piano. "If you give me ten dollars, you can have her."

The piano, old as it was, was in excellent condition. Sam played a few chords and found that it seemed to be in tune. "It's a deal, Mrs. Harper."

With the help of the Harpers' sons, Sam loaded the piano onto the wagon. Then, rejoicing in the goodness of God, he headed back to the ranch.

When Sam arrived home, he was pleased to find that Esther was down by the creek with the boys. He hoped he could sneak the piano into the house and surprise her.

"Tom! Look what God sent us!"

Tom stepped out of the house and grinned. "Praise the Lord. I don't believe it, buddy! Where in the world did you find that?"

"Tell you later. Right now, will you help me get it into the house?"

"Sure, it's a good thing you made the front door nice and wide."

"I did it for this very reason," Sam informed him.

As they were moving the piano into the house, Carol came out of the kitchen. "Oh my! Oh Sam, this is wonderful." When they had set it in the corner, they stepped back beside her to admire it.

"I can't wait until Esther sees her piano," Carol said.

Sam agreed. "I'm going to get her. Carol, will you wipe the dust off it and cover it with some blankets or something, please?"

"Yes."

Smiling broadly, Sam walked down to the water where Esther and the boys were. Duke, watching his five young charges, was there also.

Esther and the boys were sitting on the ground looking for four-leaf clovers. Sam and Esther had taught their boys that there was no magic or luck in a four-leaf clover, but it was a special thing God had created for His children to enjoy.

"Hi, Sam," Esther greeted. "Did they have everything you needed?"

Sam tried to keep a straight face. "Yep, *everything*."

He could not hide the twinkle in his green eyes. *He's up to something*, she thought.

Sam looked down at his boys sprawled on the lush green grass. "Boys, I need you to do me a favor. Go up to the house and help Aunt Carol."

"Yes sir," they chorused.

Sam watched them run and then looked back at Esther. "Did you find any four-leaf clovers?"

"No. Did you?" she asked with a teasing note in her voice.

"Kind of. Would you like to see it?" She nodded, and he took her hand and led her to the house. Once inside, Sam turned her so that she could see the instrument. Carol, Tom, and the boys pulled off the blankets.

"Oh my . . . oh my . . .," she kept saying softly. She stepped forward, laid her hands on the piano, and looked up at her husband. Tears filled her eyes and she rushed into his arms. "Sam, it's simply wonderful. I can't believe it."

He returned her embrace warmly. "I could hardly believe it either."

She kissed him and then ran back to the piano and stared at it.

"Aren't you going to play, Mom?" Matthew asked.

"Oh, yes, of course," Esther replied, still somewhat dazed. "What shall I play?"

"Your song, Mommy, your song, please," Monty pleaded. "Mom's song" was her arrangement of "At the Cross."

"Alright, Soldier." Esther sat down on the bench and laid her fingers on the keys. "Here it goes." As Esther played, the family gathered closer around the piano. After she had played the piece through once, they all joined in and sang. Not until it was time to start supper did the singing end.

"Thank you, Sam," Esther whispered. Taking hold of his arm, she started for the kitchen to prepare the meal.

"You're welcome, Esther honey."

Chapter 3

Preparing for Winter

"Yep, it can get cold here in Montana. Especially on this side of the Territory," Sheriff Elwood said. "We may not get as much snow as some places, but it does get cold sometimes. Many people have left after staying for only one winter. The wind blows across the plains and there isn't much to block it. So as you can imagine, the wind is powerful. Then of course, we do get a fair amount of snow."

"When will the first snow fly?" Tom asked.

"Come late October and early November, you best be frequently checking the sky. Course, it doesn't do any harm to start preparing now."

"What would you suggest we do to help us get through the winter?" asked Sam. It was Sunday afternoon and the two young men were at the sheriff's office seeking the wisdom of Keith Elwood. He, his wife Beverly, and their young son Ryan had lived in the Montana Territory for several years. After church that morning, he had invited them to his office to discuss winter preparations.

"Oh, the normal things you would do to make it through any winter. Stock up as many dry goods as you can and try to keep a plentiful store of meat, vegetables, and fruits. Have plenty of firewood ready and your shovels and axes handy. Keep your rifles in working order. You'll need ammunition for them. Make sure your lanterns are dependable and stock up on candles and lamp oil. It's good for the women to have lots of sewing supplies, like cloth, needles, and thread. You need plenty of warm clothing for everyone. If any of your harnesses, wagons, or saddles need repair, do it now, and keep plenty of fodder for your animals. Mend anything that looks broken around the house and barn. You get the idea. Try to figure out what needs you'll have and see what you can do to supply those things. Plan for the unexpected, too, like being completely snowed in and not being able to bring in any firewood. I like to keep about a week's worth in my cellar."

"Thank you, Sheriff, you've been very helpful," Tom said as he and Sam stood up to leave.

"You're welcome. If you have any more questions, come on back and I'll try to answer them. One more word of advice. Talk to other people in the area. See what kind of supplies they've needed during the winter months. Sam, you have more in your family than I do. You might want to talk to the Lerento family tonight after church. They have eight children and have been here for three winters."

"I'll do that. Thanks again, Sheriff." Sam and Tom had started toward the door when a small boy ran in with a terrified look on his face.

"Sheriff, Sheriff, some big boys untied Sparky from the hitching post and they won't give him back! My daddy went home to see how mommy was feeling and he won't be back until right before church. Will you please help me?" His pleading eyes looked up at the tall sheriff.

Keith winked at Sam and Tom, grabbed his hat, and said, "Come on, Al, I'll get Sparky for you."

"Oh, thank you, Sheriff," Al said, falling in step behind him. In the shadow of Keith Elwood, Al no longer appeared frightened.

Tom and Sam walked outside and watched the sheriff approach the culprits. They scattered when they saw him coming, but he collared one of them and rather gruffly said, "This is the third time I've caught the whole lot of you causing mayhem. If it happens one more time, I'll arrest you all. Maybe a couple of days in jail will teach you some manners." The boy he had hold of turned pale.

He continued, "I hope I don't have to do that, though. Now, you go on and tell your friends what I said." The boy nodded and, the minute Mr. Elwood let him go, ran down the street as fast as he could. After watching him until he disappeared into a building, Sheriff Elwood turned his attention to young Al, who had thrown his arms around the black pony's neck. Sparky nibbled at Al's sleeve, happy to be back with his young master.

"Thank you, Sheriff Elwood."

"You're welcome. Here, take this penny and go buy you some candy."

The lad thanked the sheriff again, jumped into the saddle, and headed Sparky for the general store.

"Sammy, we sure are blessed to have a sheriff that's not concerned just about big problems."

"You're right, Tom. He takes care of little ones, too."

The Goodtons and Sampsons discovered that preparing for a winter in Montana differed greatly from what they were used to.

"I just can't believe all the things that need to be done before the snow flies," Esther said, examining a "to-do list." "Back in Indiana, it seemed easy to get ready for winter."

"Back home, we had lots of friends and family who seemed to always drop in and see if we needed something," Sam reminded her. "Out here, the nearest neighbors are those in town." He swallowed the last of his coffee and, finished with his breakfast, stood up and joined her in studying the list.

"You're right," she said. "Well, what do we do first?"

"Sigh?" Sam suggested. With a laugh, they both exhaled deeply.

"Okay, I feel better," she teased. "What next?"

"First, Tom and I are going to build more shelves in the root cellar. I want to make sure we have plenty of room to store our food. Next, we'll check the house and barn and see what needs to be repaired. Then we'll all go to town and stock up on supplies. We'll come home and fix things up and store our food. After that," he paused for a moment, "I'm really not sure."

Esther laughed. "I think that will do for now. I may have to 'sigh' a few times in-between all that as it is."

So the work began. Everyone had something to do. Matthew was sent to the barn to take inventory of their feed. Mike and Mac cleaned lanterns. Esther and Carol inspected winter clothing to make sure it would protect against severe weather. The two youngest boys assisted them.

Sam and Tom went to work on the shelves.

To their surprise, the chore took only a day.

"That didn't take long." Tom wiped dust off his hands. He looked at the new shelves with satisfaction. "These will work fine."

"Yeah, and they were easy to make. I know they aren't works of beauty, but they'll do," Sam said. They blew out their lanterns and went back upstairs.

"All done," Tom announced as they walked into the kitchen.

"Wonderful," Carol said. "Just in time for supper."

The next day was spent making a list of things they needed from town. Early, Wednesday morning, taking two wagons, the families headed for Miles City. They rode in Sam's wagon, and planned to fill Tom's empty wagon with supplies.

As they were riding, Carol pulled a list out of her handbag and read it aloud. When she had finished, Sam said, "I suggest you ladies handle the food and sewing articles. We men will handle the other things." He stiffened and prayed for safety as they approached a piece of rock-strewn ground that they called Rocky-land. It was a flat place where rattlesnakes loved to lie on rocks and bathe in the sun. Rabbits that hid in the safety of the rocks would sometimes dart in front of or underneath a horse and spook it. A horse could easily step on a loose stone and either spook or fall. Sam tightened the reins on the two horses. He glanced over his shoulder to make sure Tom was doing all right.

Tom handled horses magnificently. They trusted him, and that morning was no exception. They made it across with no problem.

"Thank You, Lord," Esther said when the danger was passed. The others echoed their thanks.

Sam, relaxing a bit once they were on better ground, sat quietly and listened to the chatter of his family as they discussed the coming winter and the supplies they would need.

Sam knew they were a blessed family. Most people that came west had few possessions, little money, and could barely afford to make it through the first winter. It was not so with the Goodtons and Sampsons. Ever since Sam could remember, he had prepared for the day that he would move west. When he and Tom started farming their own land, the Lord helped them be frugal with their finances. Also, they had tied for first place in a horse race, and each had won five hundred dollars. Outside of their tithes, offerings, and purchases for the farm, most every cent they made went into the bank.

When they decided to pack up and go west, their friends and family purchased some things for them and the church gave them money. Sam and Tom were able to pay for all their supplies without using their savings. By the time they sold their stock and property, they had plenty of funds to help them get their ranch started. Sam chuckled. He would never forget the shock on the bank teller's face when he and Tom deposited their money in the First National Bank.

It was not long until they heard the sounds of the town. Soon they pulled up in front of the general store.

"We'll drop the ladies off here." Sam jumped off the wagon to help Esther down. Tom was already assisting Carol.

"Thank you, Sam," Esther replied. "Where will you guys be?"

"I'm going over to the gunsmith to have him look at my pistol," Tom said. "I'll pick up the ammunition if you want me to."

"Mommy, can we go with Uncle Tom, please?" Mac begged. Mike nodded hopefully.

"It's fine with me," Tom said.

Esther smiled down at the twins. "I don't mind, just as long as you behave and stay with Uncle Tom."

"We will," the boys promised.

With a boy holding each of his hands, Tom started for the smithy's shop.

"I'll take the wagon and get the feed that we need. I'll probably stop by the blacksmith, too," Sam told Esther. He looked at his three other sons. "What do you say boys, you want to come with me?"

Montana and Martin shouted in delight and ran to his side.

"You can come too, Matt," Sam said.

Matt grinned but shook his head. "If it's okay with you, I'll stay and help Mom."

Esther put her arm around the boy. "What would I do without my Warrior?"

Sam winked at Matthew and turned to Duke. "Here boy, get in and stay." The dog jumped into the wagon and lay down. His tail thumped up and down as if to say, "Don't worry about me, I'll lay here and enjoy the sun." Sam laughed. Duke looked like a harmless teddy bear, but if anyone tried to take the wagon, Duke would put up a fight.

Sam helped Monty and Martin into the other wagon and settled into the seat beside them.

Esther, Carol, and Matthew watched them leave and then went into the store.

"Good morning, Mrs. Kenneth," Carol greeted cheerfully.

"Good morning, Mrs. Sampson, Mrs. Goodton, and Matthew. Is that right? It is Matthew isn't it?" Linda asked. The folks in the town were still trying to remember who was who in the Goodton family.

"Yes ma'am. I'm Matthew."

"I'm glad I got it right," she said with a smile. She turned back to the two ladies. "What can I do for you?"

"We need several things, please." Carol handed her the list.

Linda glanced through it and said, "Steve and I will get this filled for you."

"Did I hear my name mentioned?" Steve asked, walking into the store.

"Yes, they have a list of supplies they need," Linda said.

Steve read the items. "I see you're getting ready for winter."

"Yes, and we were wondering if we need anything else," Esther said. "We've already talked to a few people, including the Lerento family. Do you have any other suggestions?"

"Looking at this list, I'd say you have most everything covered. There is one thing I would suggest though. Sometimes people plan for everything except for the long days and nights when they can't get out and do anything. They get what we call 'cabin fever.' Try to have some things to keep yourselves occupied, especially those boys."

"What do they like to do?" Linda asked.

"Well," Esther said, "Sam has been saving all the hides from the deer he has shot. Matt is going to braid some rope. That will keep him occupied. Mike likes to read, draw, and write. I probably should get him some more paper. Mac loves to carve and whittle. He could do that all day, and the little ones play with marbles every chance they get. As for us adults, Carol and I have lots of sewing we would like to get done and Sam and Tom are going to work on furniture. I'm sure the boys will want to help them."

"It sounds like you are well-prepared," Steve assured them.

They went to prayer meeting that evening then made their way home.

The next few days were spent making sure the house and barn would stand the winter. Since they were brand new, the task did not take long.

"Hand me that hammer, will you?" Tom asked. "Boy, my wagon horse did a number on the gate of this box stall."

"He did a number on the rat that spooked him too," Sam said. "It's a wonder we have a barn left. I told you not to buy him," he added, his face feigning anger.

Tom straightened, a twinkle in his eye. "I hate to burst your bubble, Sammy, but *you* are the one that suggested I buy that horse."

Sam looked shocked. "Me?"

Tom nearly fell over laughing as Sam added, "I know. I did suggest it. Here's the hammer." As Sam handed him the tool, he praised God for the friendship he had with Tom Sampson.

A few minutes later Sam said, "Maybe next spring we can get us two or three good stallions and mares to breed."

Tom's face lit up. "Yeah, maybe. Hey, if you could breed and raise any type of horse, what would you raise?"

Sam forked some straw into the stall for bedding before answering. "Remember that Tennessee Walker we saw a couple of years back? I'd like to raise them."

"That horse was beautiful. The only Walker I'd ever seen. I remember being awed at how smooth his gait was."

"Yeah."

"Well, Sammy, maybe one day."

"Dad, Uncle Tom, Mommy sent you some fresh cookies." The voice was Mac's and he came in with a plate of cookies.

"Just what the doctor ordered," Sam said. "Thank you, Lumberjack, and tell Mom we said thank you."

Chapter 4

Snow

Martin crawled out of bed feeling depressed. Every day for a month the first thing he had done was look to see if it had snowed. The day before had been November 2, and still no snow. He was beginning to think there would never be any that winter.

Shivering as his feet left the rug by his bed and hit the cold wood floor, he tiptoed to the window. As soon as his eyes became accustomed to the morning light, he saw it. At least two inches of snow covered the ground, and more was falling.

"Yahoo! Monty! Monty, look! It's snowing!" Forgetting the cold floor, he ran across the room to his brother's bed.

During the night Monty had made a cocoon out of his blanket, with himself in the middle. No matter how hard Martin shook him, he could not wake him. Finally, he grabbed one end of the blanket and pulled. The whole bundle fell off the bed and landed on the floor with a thud. The cocoon opened and Monty stood up sleepily. "What happened?" he asked, stifling a yawn.

Martin took his arm and led him to the window. "Look, Montana, it's snowing! Look!"

Monty, still half asleep, rubbed his eyes and looked out the window. He grinned at the sight of the falling snow. "Finally!" he cried, slapping his brother on the back. "Come on. Let's go tell the others!" Together they left their room and raced down the steps.

Sam and Esther had been in the kitchen when they heard the boys yell. Sam was coming up the stairs to check on them when they collided with him. He managed to keep them from tumbling down the steps and to maintain his own balance at the same time.

"Slow down, you two," he scolded gently. "You're going to get hurt. What's the rush anyway, and who was making all the noise?"

By that time the whole family had awakened. They had come out of their rooms and were waiting to find out what was happening.

"Is someone hurt?" Esther asked anxiously.

"It's snowing!" the two younger boys cried in unison.

"Really?" Mike asked, leaning over the rail that stretched from one staircase to the other. The three older boys went down the other staircase and threw open the door.

The four adults, who already knew about the snow, laughed softly as the boys gazed at it.

"Mommy, Daddy, can we go outside?" Mac pleaded.

"Not until after breakfast and devotions. Now go up and get dressed," Esther said.

As the boys rushed upstairs, Tom smiled and whispered, "You'd think they'd never seen snow before."

Never had five boys gotten ready so quickly. In no time at all, they had washed, changed, and were sitting at the table.

As always, morning devotions were after breakfast. Martin sat still, but Esther could tell he was fidgeting inside. As soon as the last 'amen' was said, his words tumbled out. "Mom, may I please be excused to go outside and play?"

"Yes, you may. All of you go get your winter things, and Aunt Carol and I will help you get into them."

In minutes, the boys were bundled up and ready to go. They ran outside, leapt off the porch, and rolled in the snow for a few minutes until someone threw a snowball. Whooping with enthusiasm, they all scooped up handfuls of snow and the fight began.

During the middle of the game, a stray snowball hit Duke in the shoulder. "Duke, I'm sorry," Mike said, running over to the dog. "Are you okay?" Duke lowered his head and tucked his tail between his legs. When Mike bent over to hug him and beg his forgiveness, Duke knocked him down, pinned him in the snow, and began to lick him.

"Oh, Duke, you tricked me!" Mike cried after he had wiggled out from beneath him, but his face glowed with delight. "Come on, Duke, see if you can catch me."

Esther and Carol watched them from inside the house. "I'm glad the boys are having fun," Esther said.

Just then Sam and Tom appeared, decked out in their winter clothing.

"What are you guys going to do?" Esther asked.

"I think it's a shame to waste the first good snow of the year," Sam said. "Don't you?" He kissed her cheek and went out the door.

"What can I say?" Tom asked, making sure his hat was snug. "Looks like fun to me." He kissed Carol and followed Sam.

Carol doubled over with laughter as she watched the seven "boys" and the dog play in the snow. "Isn't that a sight!" she said when she finally caught her breath.

Esther smiled warmly. "Yes, a wonderful sight. Well, what do you think?"

"About what?"

"Shall we join them?"

Carol's eyes sparkled. "Why not?"

The week wore on, and the temperature grew colder and colder. What had begun as fun became frustrating. The snow piled so high that every morning Tom and Sam had to shovel a path from the house to the barn.

"You know, Sam," Tom began on Saturday morning. His shovel was full and he threw the snow off to his right. "We ought to attach a rope from the house to the barn. If the snow was to get so thick that we couldn't see, we might not be able to reach the barn to feed the animals."

"Good idea, Tommy. Matt already has a good length of that rope he's been braiding. He'd be pleased to know that we'll use it for something important."

"There he is now," Tom nodded toward the house.

Matthew had left the porch and was coming toward them, shovel in hand. "Good morning, Dad, Uncle Tom. Can I help?"

"Sure, Matt. We could use your help," Sam told him.

As they worked, Sam asked about using the ropes for a safety line. Matt stopped shoveling and studied the distance between the house and the barn. "I'm pretty sure that it'll reach," he said. "Want me to run and get it?"

"Yes."

Matthew laid down his shovel and raced back into the house. "Mom, would you get my ropes for me, please? I don't want to track in any snow."

"I'll get them," Montana volunteered.

"I only need the long one."

"Okay." Montana hurried to the room where the ropes were stored.

"What do you need it for, Matt?" Esther asked.

"Dad and Uncle Tom want to put a safety line from the house to the barn. They want to use my rope."

Esther smiled at Matt's thrill that his father was going to use the ropes he had worked hard on. "That's a very good idea."

Monty came around the corner with the once neatly rolled rope now in an ugly tangle. "Here you go, Matty."

"What happened?" Matthew asked.

"I pulled it off the hook."

"Monty, I had them rolled so nicely..."

"Boys, wait a minute. Matthew, don't get angry with him and Montana, next time be more careful and lift it off the hook."

"Yes, Momma. I'm sorry, Matty."

"That's okay; I'm sorry, too. Thanks for getting it."

Esther helped Matthew roll it back up and the young boy ran outside. "Here it is, Dad. Do you want me to tie one end to the porch?"

"Yeah, tie the line like I taught you. Make sure it's secure."

"Yes, sir." He was silent for a few minutes as he tied the rope. "All secure, Dad." He began to walk toward them, letting out the line of rope along the way. The path was clear of snow, and Matt was able to walk all the way to the barn. Once there, he tied the other end of the rope to a metal loop that Sam had nailed into the wall.

"There, that's perfect," Tom said, giving the line a tug. "That'll hold good." He ran his hand along the rope. "Matty, this is excellent. I don't know that I've ever seen a finer job."

"Thank you, Uncle Tom. Dad and Grandpa Maker taught me how to do it."

Toward evening, the family began thinking about Sunday church services.

"Do you think we'll be able to go to church tomorrow, Sam?" Esther was looking out the window. They had missed Wednesday night because of the severe weather.

Sam gazed out at the sky. "I think we will. It looks like the weather will hold." He turned to Tom. "What do you think?"

"I think we can."

Sunday morning skies were clear and the air was crisp. They bundled up, had prayer, and headed for town. Arriving safely, they saw

other families making their way to church. On
summer days, people walked slowly, enjoying
the sun and fellowship with their friends, but
this morning they walked briskly, hurrying their
children along.

Tom, Carol, Sam, Esther, and the boys
were among the first to get there. The fire in
the wood stove sent out comforting warmth,
making it easier to take off their wraps.

"Have a good time in Sunday School,"
Esther told the boys as they went to their
classes.

"Yes, ma'am," the boys chorused.

The adults made their way to the second
row of the auditorium. It was a small church,
seating about one hundred people. The
Goodtons waved to those they knew and
watched with pleasure as the building filled up.

After Sunday school, the children joined
their parents in the auditorium. Soon it was
time for the preaching. Pastor McBride stood
behind the pulpit and asked the people to turn
to Luke 16:19-31.

"Folks," he said, "today I'm going to preach
on a very unpleasant subject—hell. Despite
what some people say, hell is a real place filled
with real fire. It is not a subject that people like

to talk about. In fact, quite often people speak lightly of it, but Jesus never did. In the book of Luke, the Lord tells us about two men. One went to paradise and the other went to hell. Often, Jesus would use parables to illustrate a principle but never in a parable did He use a proper name. In this account, He does. So, that tells us that this is not a parable. This account is about two men who literally lived and died. Let's read from Luke chapter sixteen, starting in verse nineteen." The pastor gave everyone time to find the passage before he began to read.

"There was a certain rich man, which was clothed in purple and fine linen, and fared sumptuously every day:

"And there was a certain beggar named Lazarus, which was laid at his gate, full of sores,

"And desiring to be fed with the crumbs which fell from the rich man's table: moreover the dogs came and licked his sores.

"And it came to pass, that the beggar died, and was carried by the angels into

Abraham's bosom: the rich man also died, and was buried;

"And in hell he lift up his eyes, being in torments, and seeth Abraham afar off, and Lazarus in his bosom.

"And he cried and said, Father Abraham, have mercy on me, and send Lazarus, that he may dip the tip of his finger in water, and cool my tongue; for I am tormented in this flame.

"But Abraham said, Son, remember that thou in thy lifetime receivedst thy good things, and likewise Lazarus evil things: but now he is comforted, and thou art tormented.

"And beside all this, between us and you there is a great gulf fixed: so that they which would pass from hence to you cannot; neither can they pass to us, that would come from thence.

"Then he said, I pray thee therefore, father, that thou wouldest send him to my father's house:

"For I have five brethren; that he may testify unto them, lest they also come into this place of torment.

"Abraham saith unto him, They have Moses and the prophets; let them hear them.

"And he said, Nay, father Abraham: but if one went unto them from the dead, they will repent.

"And he said unto him, If they hear not Moses and the prophets, neither will they be persuaded, though one rose from the dead."

The pastor stopped reading and looked at the congregation. "The first thing I want to say is, the wicked shall be cast into hell. The Bible says in Psalms 9:17, 'The wicked shall be turned into hell, and all the nations that forget God.' Some people may not know what hell really is. Hell is a place that was prepared for the devil and his angels. We learn this in Matthew 25:41, which says, 'Then shall he say also unto them on the left hand, Depart from me, ye cursed, into everlasting fire, prepared for the devil and his angels:'

"Hell was not made for men. But when man sinned in the garden, he brought upon himself the penalty of death, and not only death, but eternity in hell.

"Hell is a place filled with fire. Mark 9:46 says it is a place 'where their worm dieth not, and the fire is not quenched.' And according to II Peter 2:4, hell is a place of darkness: 'For if God spared not the angels that sinned, but cast them down to hell, and delivered them into chains of darkness, to be reserved unto judgment;'

"Those in hell will be there for eternity. In Matthew 25:46, Jesus declares that lost men 'shall go away into everlasting punishment: but the righteous into life eternal.'

"People often ask me, 'How could a loving God send people to hell?' My second point is, God has *never* sent anyone to hell.

"God does not want people to go to hell. The Bible says in Ezekiel 33:11, 'Say unto them, As I live, saith the Lord GOD, I have no pleasure in the death of the wicked; but that the wicked turn from his way and live: turn ye, turn ye from your evil ways;'

"God gave the best that Heaven had, Jesus Christ, to purchase salvation so that you and I would not have to go to hell. Jesus, the only begotten Son of God, left Heaven and came to earth, robed in human flesh. He lived a perfect life and could have gone back to Heaven and said, 'I lived perfectly, so I don't have to die.' If He had, though, we could never have been saved. So He willingly went to the cross, shed His blood, and died to forgive our sins and purchase salvation. All we have to do to get salvation is simply repent and believe on Jesus. Salvation is very simple, and it is for everyone.

"If you don't get saved, you'll die and go to hell, and you'll not be able to blame it on God. He has done everything He can to show you that He loves you and that He wants you to be saved. All you must do is ask Him to save you. Can't you see His love for you? Can't you see Him standing between you and hell, His arms stretched out, begging you to come to Him and be saved?

"Which brings me to my last point. If you go to hell, you will have to tread underfoot the Son of God. II Peter 3:9 says, 'The Lord is not slack concerning his promise, as some men count slackness; but is longsuffering to us-ward, not willing that any should perish, but that all should come to repentance.'"

The pastor paused for a moment and looked out over the congregation. He knew that several people in the auditorium were lost.

In the back, a row of cowpunchers had come to the services simply out of curiosity. Three of them were under great conviction. One was gripping the back of the pew in front of him with so much force that his knuckles were white. To the pastor's left sat a young couple who professed to be Christians, but the wife was not living like one. She was fidgeting nervously. A teenage boy and girl near the front were crying softly. Their father was lost, and that morning was the first time he had come to church.

Pastor McBride began to speak. "I'm not glad there is a hell, but just because I wish there wasn't one doesn't make hell disappear. And just because you choose not to believe in hell doesn't make the fires burn any less. You're like a child when he's hiding. Sometimes he'll stick his head behind a pillow and think that because he can't see you, you can't see him, but it's not true. Hell is real! It will always be real! The only way to escape it is to hide yourself in the precious blood of Jesus Christ. Please bow your heads and close your eyes."

The pianist began to play as the invitation started.

"My friend, if you are lost, today can be the day that you get it settled. Second Corinthians 6:2 says, 'behold, now is the accepted time; behold, now is the day of salvation.' You could leave this place knowing you are on your way to Heaven. I'm going to close in prayer. When I'm done, if you're lost, come right down here to the front and we'll get someone to take a Bible and show you how you can be saved. If you are saved, come and pray for your lost loved ones."

After the pastor had prayed, many people made their way to the altar. Mac was trying to calm his racing heart. All during the service, he had been afraid. He had never asked the Lord to save him, and he knew that if he died he would go to hell. He wanted to get saved. He looked for his father and mother, but they were both at the altar; his father leading one of the cowboys to Christ and his mother helping the young wife. Mac looked for the pastor, but he was dealing with the father of the two teenagers. Uncle Tom and Aunt Carol were at the altar, too.

Mac once again looked around for someone to help him. His eyes rested upon Matthew.

Matthew will know how to help me, he thought. His brother was on the other end of the pew. MacShane quickly crawled over three of his brothers and grabbed Matt's hand. "Matty," he cried in his brother's ear, "I need to get saved!"

Matthew took his Bible and led Mac to the altar. They knelt, and Matthew opened his Bible to Romans 3:23 and read, "For all have sinned, and come short of the glory of God;" Turning a few pages, he read Romans 6:23: "For the wages of sin is death; but the gift of God is eternal life through Jesus Christ our Lord."

"These verses say that everyone has sinned and that the penalty for sin is death," Matt explained. "Do you know what sin is, Mac?"

"Yes, it's the bad things that we do."

"That's right. Are you willing to admit to God that you are a sinner?"

Mac nodded.

"Okay, let's go to Romans 5:8. 'But God commendeth his love toward us, in that, while we were yet sinners, Christ died for us.' Like the pastor said, Jesus died to pay for our sins and to purchase salvation for you and me.

Salvation involves two things, repentance and faith. Repentance is agreeing with God. Faith is putting your trust in what Jesus did on the cross to forgive your sins. The Bible says in Romans 10:9 and 13, 'That if thou shalt confess with thy mouth the Lord Jesus, and shalt believe in thine heart that God hath raised him from the dead, thou shalt be saved. . . . For whosoever shall call upon the name of the Lord shall be saved.'"

Matt looked up. "Mac," he said gently, "you said you wanted to get saved. Do you know what to do?"

"Yes, I need to tell God I'm a sinner and ask Jesus to save me."

"That's right."

Mac closed his eyes and began to pray. "Dear Jesus, I know I'm a sinner, but I'd like to get saved. Thank You, Jesus, for dying on the cross for me. I don't want to go to hell. Please save me. Thank You, Jesus, thank You." He looked up at his brother. "He saved me, Matt. He did. Just like He promised."

Matt smiled and the two brothers embraced.

Chapter 5

The Meadowlark

Spring came, bringing with it the beauty of new life. Sam and Tom had already sectioned off a piece of land that they wanted to seed. Until they could buy a herd of cattle, they would plant a crop.

"Where are the boys, Esther?" Carol asked. It was an exceptionally warm day, despite the wind, and they were sitting on the porch doing some mending and planning their gardening schedule.

"Well, they're scattered far and abroad." Esther's eyes sparkled when she thought of her children. "I think I saw Matthew and Duke head toward the forest. The twins are in the barn with Uncle Tom. Marty and Monty are inside, but I suspect that they'll be out soon. I tell you, I can hardly keep those two inside." At that moment the door flew open and the two boys ran outside.

"Hi, Mom, we're going to the barn." Monty took a flying leap off the porch.

"Beat you there!" Martin cried, passing Monty as they raced toward the barn. His older brother ran for all he was worth to catch up.

Esther watched the two boys enter the barn. "Oh my. I can hardly keep up with Martin." She chuckled. "I hope he slows down one of these days."

A few minutes later they saw Matthew running up to them.

"Mom, Mom! Come quick!"

Esther jumped up and hurried to him. "What is it, Matthew?"

"I . . . found . . . it," he said, trying to catch his breath.

"Found what?"

"It's the first flower I've found this year! Come on, I'll show you!" He grabbed her hand and pulled her toward the edge of the forest. Together they ran for a few hundred yards. Suddenly, Matt stopped.

"There, Mom. Look." A bitterroot stood alone with grass and snow forming a green and white backdrop. The flower looked tired, as if standing against the winter winds was about to destroy it.

"Oh, Matt, it's beautiful!" Esther knelt beside it and fingered the pink petals gently. "It's lovely. I'm surprised that it's blooming this early." She sat up, thought for a minute, and said, "Matthew, go back to the house and get my garden shovel and a small pot."

Her instructions caught him off guard, but he ran off to carry out her orders. He returned shortly with the shovel and pot and laid the tools beside her.

"Here, Mom. What do you need these for?"

"I'm going to dig this flower up and put it in the house until summer. Inside, it will get all the sunshine and water that it needs. When I get my flower garden planted, we'll put it in there. If it stays out here, it'll die. Look at it. It's not very old and already it's dying." She made a circle the size of the pot around the flower and carefully dug below its roots. Lifting the ball of dirt, she set it in the pot. "There. Now, let's get this flower out of the cold."

Matthew volunteered to carry the plant, and they went back to the house.

"Where should I set it, Mom?"

"Let's see…I know, the kitchen window. There it'll get lots of sun and attention." Esther led the way, and Matt set it where it could get the most sun.

"Perfect," Esther praised. "You know what I think?" She put her arm around her son. "I think that, because this is a special flower, it ought to have a name. What do you think?"

Matt grinned. Lately, his mother wanted to have a name for everything. Sam had begun teasing her by saying she had all the china named, and promptly she would pretend to recite their names to him.

The boy turned his attention back to the flower. "A name . . . hmm . . . Since spring is kind of the season of hope, why don't we call it Hope?"

"Hope, the bitterroot. I like it. Hope will really brighten up the kitchen, don't you think?"

April came and the men planted the crops in the first two weeks. It was such a relief on that last Wednesday to know that all the crops were in before the rains came. At church, they were pleased to know that everyone else had also got their crops planted.

That Thursday, Tom said, "Sam, Carol and I are going to start building our house. Now seems like a good time."

Sam, working on the corral gate, looked at him. "Tommy, you know that you and Carol are welcome to stay with us."

Tom smiled. "Yeah, we know, and we appreciate it, too. We need a place of our own, though. Well, Carol needs a place of her own. You know what I mean. Her own kitchen and decorations and such. It's important to her. Not that we both haven't been happy with you all. It's been a lot of fun, but I think we need to start on our own house."

Sam nodded. "I understand, Tom."

The next day they made their way to the lumberyard.

"Look who's back," Jeff said when they jumped out of the wagon in front of his shop. "What can I do for you?"

"I'm ready to start building my house," Tom told him. "I've worked out the amount of lumber I need." He handed his figures to Jeff.

"I can get that for you tomorrow, if you like. Me and my men will bring it out to your place."

"Thanks, I sure do appreciate that. Just bring the lumber to Sam's house. Our house won't be far from his. Oh, and if you don't mind, I'd like to pay for it now."

"That'll be fine. Give me a minute to figure it up." Jeff quickly worked out the total and handed Tom the bill. After Tom paid it, he and Sam went over to the general store.

"Howdy, Mr. Kenneth," Sam greeted.

"Good morning to you! What can I do for you?"

"I'm going to build a house," Tom explained. "Here are some things that I need."

"Okay." Steve began to fill Tom's order. "Say, did you boys hear about the railroad coming?" Sam and Tom leaned over the counter anxiously.

"No, what about it?" Sam asked.

"Well, already it's extended to Sioux Falls, South Dakota. That's roughly about 700 miles away. They're saying that it might be all the way to Miles City before the snow flies this winter. And if that happens, business will really pick up around here. Cattlemen will start herding their cattle here to ship them out east. More people will move out here. This place will start growing by leaps and bounds!"

Sam and Tom looked at one other. Each knew what the other was thinking. Maybe next spring they could buy a herd of cattle. They planned to purchase the cattle out of state and ship the bulls home and drive the rest. Then they could really get their ranch started.

"That's not all," Steve continued. "Sheriff Elwood says that the army will be coming up here to guide the surveying team. Apparently, the railroad has met with some opposition. A couple of the tracks have been blown up and someone has been taking shots at the workers."

"I wonder why anyone wouldn't want the railroad to come out here," Sam wondered aloud.

"There's most always a few people who don't want any kind of modern change to take place, but they're usually not dangerous," Tom said. "I wonder who would be fighting it."

"You boys have to remember something. The railroad could put the stage and freight lines out of business. That in itself will get some people angry. And it will bring the army, and that don't set well with the outlaws," Steve explained. "We don't have too much trouble with outlaws here. We've got a mighty good sheriff, but there are limits to his jurisdiction. He can only chase them while they're inside his boundaries. The army has fewer boundaries, and they won't have to stop when the outlaws cross into the next county. Well, here are your supplies and the bill."

"Thanks." While Tom paid the storekeeper, Sam began to load the wagon. Soon they were on their way home.

"I can hardly believe that it could be as soon as next spring that we can get our first herd," Tom said eagerly.

"That will be quite a relief. I've been thinking. Maybe we should hire some men to start building fences on our ranges."

"That's a good idea. Maybe Jeff could round us up a couple of fellows." Tom tightened the reins. The horses were frisky, and he had to keep them in check.

The next day, Jeff and his men came, bringing the lumber. As before, they stayed and helped with the building.

Just before lunchtime on the fourth day, Esther, Carol, and Terry Ray were preparing the food when Carol said suddenly, "Listen." A bird was making a flute-like sound. "I've heard that bird many times since we've come to Montana," she said

"You'll hear lots more," Terry said. "That's a Western Meadowlark. They're all over the place." Terry listened to determine which direction the sound was coming from. "There," she said, pointing, and the others followed her gaze. A brown bird, with a yellow belly and a black yoke around its neck, perched on a bush, singing cheerfully.

"He's lovely!" Carol exclaimed. "What kind of bird did you say it was?"

"Western Meadowlark," Terry said again.

Tom and Carol's house was not as big as Sam and Esther's so with everyone working hard, the house was finished on the twenty-seventh.

"Well, Carol, what do you think?" Tom asked on their first night in the new house.

Carol looked around her and smiled. "I couldn't have dreamed of anything better."

The design was simple. To the left of the front door was a window, and beyond that the parlor. Past the parlor was the kitchen, furnished with a stove, cabinets, a sink, a pump, and a small table. To the right of the door was Tom and Carol's bedroom. Between it and the guest room was a door leading outside. On the back side, of the house, were three rooms—on the left a washroom, in the middle the sewing room, and on the right what Tom called "the big room." It took up most of that side of the house. A picture window almost covered one wall, and a door led outside. The room contained a rocking chair, a table, some straight-back chairs, a stove, a desk and chair.

In the center, of the house, was a large dining table. Above it hung a chandelier that Tom had bought from a couple planning to head farther west.

Tom put his arms around his wife. "It's not much, Carol. About the only thing fancy in here is the chandelier and even that didn't cost me much. I wish I could give you more."

She turned to look him in the eye. "Tommy, I think this place is fit for a king, but even if it were lined with gold it wouldn't mean as much to me as you do."

Tears filled Tom's eyes. "It ought to have a name. What do you think?"

Carol thought for a moment. "Of course! Why don't we call it the Meadowlark?"

"The Meadowlark," Tom repeated. "I think that's simply perfect. Our verse could be Psalms 91:4 where it says, 'He shall cover thee with his feathers, and under his wings shalt thou trust...'"

Tom suddenly grinned. "Come on!" He grabbed her hand and ran out to the porch.

"Thomas Joel Sampson, what are you doing?" Carol cried in mock anger as they stepped into the night air.

"I just realized that I never carried you across the threshold." Before she even had time to agree, Tom lifted her into his arms and carried her into the house. Once inside they both began to chuckle.

"I love you, Thomas Joel Sampson."

"And I love you, Mrs. Thomas Joel Sampson," he told her, gently letting her down and kissing her as he kicked the door shut with his foot.

Chapter 6

An Interesting Encounter

It was May 1, and Esther was preparing to bake.

"Sam, I'm nearly out of flour. Do you think you could go to town and get some for me? I've got enough to last me until you can get back."

"I can, Esther honey. Go ahead and make up a list for me, and I'll ride over to Tom's and see if they need anything."

"Dad, could I ride over there, please?" Matthew held his breath. "I promise to be careful."

"Alright, but go gently. There's no need to rush."

"Thanks, Dad!" Matt took his hat and raced toward the barn. In a few minutes, he had Dusty, Sam's old horse, saddled and bridled. Grabbing hold of the horn, he scrambled into the saddle. He waved to his parents, who were standing on the porch, and loped out of the yard. Duke followed him.

Sam and Esther watched. For a few minutes, he was out of their sight but they relaxed when they saw him emerge from the trees and trot up to the porch of Tom and Carol's house where he spoke to Tom. Tom stepped into the house, came back out, and handed him something. Matthew got back in the saddle, and soon he was back at the Silver Arrow.

"Here's the list, Dad. Uncle Tom wondered if you needed someone to go with you. If you do, wave your hat twice. If not, wave it once."

"Thanks, Matt." Sam looked over at Tom's place and saw him waiting on the porch. Sam took off his hat and waved it once. Tom waved back and went into the house.

Sam placed his hat back on his head and set out for the barn. He and Matt hitched the team to the wagon and he drove it back to the house.

"Okay, I'll be back soon. Take care." He leaned down to kiss his wife.

"You be careful too," Esther said, smiling up at him.

"Will do." He gathered the reins in his hands and slapped them across the horses' backs. "Get up."

The trip into town was lonely, and Sam wished he had taken one of the boys with him. "Next time I'll remember," he said aloud. "Come on, fellows. Let's pick up the pace." The horses responded, quickening their gait.

Sam arrived in town a short time later. The store was busy, so checking his watch and realizing he had time to wait awhile, he decided to see if Sheriff Elwood had heard anything about the railroad. He was almost to the office when he heard a man call, "Excuse me, sir. Excuse me, please." Sam took a few more steps before he realized that the man was talking to him. He turned to find a nicely dressed man in his late twenties running up to him.

"Pardon me, sir, but are you Sam Goodton?"

"Yes, I am. Do I know you?" Sam asked, trying to place him.

"No, but I know a good friend of yours. Todd Leonard."

"Todd! You know Todd Leonard?" When Sam and Tom lived in Indiana, Todd and his family had lived in the same town. Todd, Tom, and Sam were best friends. For health reasons, the Leonards had left Indiana and returned to Maine, their home state. Though they were far away, God had allowed the boys to stay in touch. They had even been able to see each other a few times. One of Todd's sisters had married Terry Carson, the son of their pastor in Indiana, and Todd had married Carol's sister, Tessa. Todd ran one of the largest shipping industries in Maine.

"I sure do know Todd. I sailed with him for a short time. The name's Philips, Mark Philips." He held out his hand.

"Well, I sure am pleased to meet you, Mr. Philips," Sam said, shaking his hand heartily. "If you have the time, I'll buy you a cup of coffee. I'd like to hear how Todd and his family are doing."

"Sounds great!"

They went into a small café and got a table.

"I met Todd when I was twenty-four," Mark explained. "After sailing with him for a year, I got the urge to head west. Captain Leonard asked that if I ever saw you to tell you 'hi,' and that they sure do miss you. He described you very well. I knew when I saw you that you had to be Sam Goodton."

Sam grinned. His height, broad shoulders, and fire red hair were hard to miss. "I'm glad you introduced yourself. How are Todd and Tessa?"

"Oh, they're doing fine. Would you believe that she had triplets?"

"Triplets!"

"Yeah, three beautiful girls. Hannah, Kathleen, and Naomi."

"How about that." Sam smiled and took a drink of coffee. "Tell me, Mr. Philips, what brought you out to Miles City?"

"I'm working for the railroad. Among other things, my superiors sent me out here to look over the land and decide where the best place for the tracks would be."

"Interesting. I hear that some of the surveyors have been treated none too gently. Any idea who might be causing all the trouble?"

"I can't really go into detail, but I will tell you this. Things are getting really rough. I have a friend in the army, and he and I have been working together. Speaking of which, I'm supposed to meet him here sometime soon. He wasn't sure of the exact day he could get here. You haven't seen him by chance have you?"

"What's his name and what does he look like?"

"His name is Tony Glen. He's about my height, dark complexioned, and—wait a minute. I think I have a picture of him." He pulled out his wallet and looked through it. "Here he is. This was taken at our family Christmas. He's the only one in a uniform."

Sam leaned across the table to get the picture and then settled back in his chair to study it. He suddenly stiffened.

"What's wrong?" Mark asked, fear gripping his heart as he wondered if something had happened to his soldier friend.

"This . . . this man . . . looks . . . like . . . like my father-in-law!" Sam explained, the words coming out slowly and full of surprise.

Mark laughed, thinking that Sam was making a joke, but Sam was not laughing. "You're serious aren't you?" Mark asked.

"I am! I have a son who looks more like him than he does me, and even he and my wife look alike. What did you say his name was?"

"Glen, Tony Glen."

"Do you know if he has any relationship with the Maker family?"

Mark thought for a moment. "Not that I recall. If he did, it would be distant, and even then it wouldn't have any affect on his looks. He was adopted. He told me that his real parents didn't want him, so the midwife gave him to the Glen family." Mark paused. "Maybe his real family was related to the Makers."

"As far as I know, none of the Makers have given up one of their children. Mark, I sure would like to meet this man."

Mark nodded. "Today is Saturday. I know for sure that he'll be here by Tuesday. If you like, meet me here on Tuesday at, say, ten o'clock?"

"I'll be here. I'd best be getting back to my ranch. You're welcome to come have dinner with us, Mark."

"Thanks, but I want to be here when Tony arrives. It sure was nice to meet you, Mr. Goodton."

"Same here," Sam replied, shaking his new friend's hand.

All the way home, Sam pondered on the likeness between Esther, Montana, Mr. Maker, and Tony Glen.

"How can such resemblance be simply coincidental?" Sam asked aloud. "I wonder if he is related to Esther, and if he is, how?" His eyes widened and he brought the horses to a stop as a thought so profound came to his mind that it frightened him. "No . . . it . . . it couldn't be," he told himself. "Then again, what if it is? No, it couldn't be!" he argued, but that nagging "what if" would not leave him alone.

"Dear Lord," he prayed, "something that I can't explain has happened. I pray that You'll give me wisdom to know how to deal with this."

He clucked to the horses and they headed down the trail again. He began to review what he knew about his wife's older brothers. It was not much. "Maybe I should ask her about them," he said to himself. Talk of her deceased brothers saddened Esther, but this was important and he would have to talk to her about it.

He stopped at Tom's house first and gave him the supplies he had asked for. Then he went home and after leaving the items at the house, he put the horses away.

As he and Esther were carrying things into the kitchen, he brought up the subject.

"Esther . . . ," he began, searching for the right words, "what do you know about your brothers?"

Esther, surprised at his question, paused in her work. "Well," she said slowly, turning to lift a parcel onto a shelf, "Mac, the oldest, was stillborn. Mother had trouble through the whole pregnancy and the baby was a month early. The doctor had feared that the baby was already gone, and he was right. Shane, the next boy, is still somewhat of a mystery. Everything seemed to go well until Mom began to deliver. There were complications. The cord was wrapped around his neck and Mother had to fight hard to deliver him. He finally came, and the doctor said that he was very healthy, but the strain nearly killed my mother. The doctor, knowing my mom needed immediate attention, gave Shane to the midwife to care for until Mom got better. For two weeks, my mother lay at death's door, but the Lord healed her, and to everyone's surprise she completely recovered." Esther sighed. "When they asked the midwife to bring Shane to them, she told them that he had died a few days before. She said that he had taken sick and there was nothing she could do. The midwife took them to the cemetery where she had buried him. Mother never even got to hold Shane." A tear trickled down Esther's cheek. "That's all there is, Sammy."

Sam nodded gently. "I see. Do you know the name of the midwife?"

"Oh, let me see here . . . It had something to do with a bush. Um . . . ," Esther tapped her fingers on the counter as she tried to remember. "Or was it a rose? Rosebush, no... Thornbush, no . . . Rose, Thorn, no . . . Oh, I remember. It was Thornberry, Elmira Thornberry!"

"Thornberry. Does she still live where your parents used to live?"

"No, she was reprimanded by the doctor for not telling them that Shane was sick and for burying the child without telling my parents. My mom told me that it took a long time for them to forgive her. As far as I know, the midwife and her husband moved away right after it all happened. As to where, I have no idea. Mom and Dad tried to find her to tell her that they were sorry for getting angry at her and that they forgave her, but they never could locate her." Esther paused. "Then some time later I was born."

"I see."

Esther studied Sam closely. She wondered if there was a reason behind his questions, but since he obviously did not want to talk about it, she did not pry. She knew that he would tell her in good time.

On Sunday, Mark was at their church but he shook his head when Sam glanced his way. Tony Glen was not there yet.

It was hard for Sam to concentrate on his work. He told Tom about Tony Glen, but asked him to keep it a secret until Sam could find out who he was.

"Do you think that he's related to Esther?" Tom asked softly. Sam and Tom, with the help of fifteen other men, were putting a fence around their property. Tom, his hands protected by gloves, pulled the wire taunt as Sam nailed it to the post.

"It sure looks like it," Sam whispered back.

Tom looked at his friend. "Do you think maybe both him and Esther were adopted? Esther by the Makers and Tony by the Glens?"

"No, she looks too much like her mother, and this Glen fellow looks like a taller version of Mr. Maker," Sam explained.

"It was just an idea. What are you going to do?"

Sam waited until one of the men passed by before he answered. "I'm not sure. Tomorrow, Lord willing, I'm going to meet him and go from there."

On Tuesday, Sam told Esther, "There's a man I have to talk to in town today. I shouldn't be gone too long."

Esther was sure that something unusual was going on, but she trusted Sam and knew that whatever he was doing was right. She hugged him. "Alright, Sam. Be careful."

"I will." He leaned down and kissed her before heading out the door.

"Dad, can I go with you?" Montana asked.

Sam wanted to take the boy with him but he shook his head. "I'm sorry, Soldier, but Daddy needs to go alone. You could help me get saddled up though."

"Okay," he answered, trying to hide his disappointment.

Sam soon had his horse saddled, in spite of Montana's "help" and was riding to Miles City.

All the way, Sam prayed, asking for wisdom and guidance. Two verses from the book of Proverbs came to his mind: "Trust in the

LORD with all thine heart; and lean not unto thine own understanding. In all thy ways acknowledge him, and he shall direct thy paths." He prayed and told God that he trusted in Him to see the situation through.

He walked into the café at ten o'clock. It was full of men in uniform, but Sam picked out Tony Glen immediately. The sight took Sam's breath away. The man, in his mid-thirties, stood up to greet him. Seen face to face, he looked even more like the Makers.

"You must be Tony Glen," Sam said.

Chapter 7

Waiting

“I am,” Tony replied, shaking Sam's hand, “and you must be Sam Goodton. My friend tells me that you claim I look like part of your family.”

“I do. Let's sit down and I'll show you.”

Once they were seated, Sam reached into his vest pocket and pulled out a picture of Esther and her family. He laid it down in front of Tony Glen.

Tony looked at the picture and swallowed hard. “T—To look at this man here,” he stuttered, pointing to Mr. Maker, “i—is like looking at me in the future.” He looked up at Sam. “You weren't kidding were you?”

Sam shook his head. “No, Mr. Glen, I wasn't. Do you mind telling me about yourself?”

“I don't mind. My adopted parents were both only children. In fact, as far as I know, I'm the only man alive that bears the name of Glen. Anyway, they couldn't have any children and it broke their hearts. They were getting ready to move from Michigan, to Illinois when a midwife friend of theirs brought me to them. She said that my real parents didn't want me and had asked her to find a good home for me." He looked again at the picture. "Maybe these people know who my real family is. Mom and Dad didn't know them. I've wanted to find out who they are." He took a deep breath. "Both my parents died a few years ago, and like I said, as far as I know I'm the only Glen left. It's kind of lonely."

Sam could not ignore the thought that had come to him on the way home from town a few days earlier.   Though it seemed impossible, he could not dismiss it. *Please help, Lord*, he prayed.

"Mr. Glen, how old are you?"

"Thirty-six."

He's the right age, Sam thought. "What is your birth date?"

"The midwife told my adopted parents that I was born on the twentieth of April."

He's got the right birth date! One more question and, well, it could mean . . . "Mr. Glen, do you know the name of the midwife?"

"Oh sure. Her name was Elmira Thornberry. Mom and I kept in touch with her for many years."

Sam nearly fell off his chair. Was it really true?

"Sir, if I'm right, what I'm about to tell you is going to change all of our lives forever." He related what Esther had told him about Shane. When he was finished, it was Tony's turn to be astonished.

"You and Shane were born on the same day and delivered by the same midwife. Both the Makers and the Glens lived in the same town. Shane supposedly died, and all of a sudden Mrs. Thornberry has a baby to give away." Sam looked Tony in the eye. "I don't think that's just a coincidence."

"Then . . . then I . . . I'm really Shane Maker, and . . . and I was stolen from my real family?" He shook his head. "No! I *refuse* to believe that my parents would ever be part of a kidnapping."

"Me too, but I also refuse to believe that the Makers would give up a son. Still, that leaves at least one possible suspect. Elmira Thornberry."

Tony nodded. "I guess she could have lied to both my parents and the Makers, but why would she?"

"I don't know. Do you have any idea if she's alive and where she lives?"

"As a matter of fact, I do! Like I said, Mom and her stayed in touch. Momma loved to send her pictures of me. I used to send her little notes, too, but after Mom passed away," he stopped and wiped away a tear, "I stopped writing to her. Now let me think . . . Where did she live?" He leaned back in his chair, deep in thought. Suddenly, he snapped his fingers. "She and her husband live in Minneapolis, Minnesota."

Sam was elated. He could find out for sure if Tony was his wife's brother. He began to form a plan, but Tony was way ahead of him.

"If we took the stage from here to Rapid City, South Dakota, then took the stage to Sioux Falls, from there we could take the train to Minneapolis."

"How long would that take?" Sam asked.

Mark knew the distances between the towns and was already figuring. "From here to Rapid City is 229 miles. Stage travels, biding any problems, a good fifty, sixty miles a day.

That'll take four to five days. Then from Rapid City to Sioux Falls is 371 miles, so that would be somewhere around six to eight days, and from Sioux Falls to Minneapolis is 280 miles. On the train, that won't take more than a day."

"Around thirty days round trip," Sam mused. "That's a long time. I need to pray about it and see what I ought to do."

"I can't go right now anyway since I have a job to complete. We've got to get this land surveyed for the railroad. With Mark and me working at it full tilt, perhaps we can get it done quickly."

"Will you be needing any help with your surveying?" Sam asked.

Tony and Mark looked at each other. They seemed to be having a silent conversation. After what seemed like a long time, Mark nodded.

Tony leaned forward and said softly, "Sam, your help would be greatly appreciated, but, Mark and I will be doing more than surveying, although that is our job."

At first, Sam was confused as he contemplated what Glen had told him. He settled back in his chair and took a good long look at the two men sitting at the table. When he first met Mark Philips, he had the distinct feeling that he had heard that name before, but with all the excitement over Tony he had forgotten about Mark. For some reason, he associated the name with the ocean and a farewell party. Suddenly he remembered. Todd Leonard had mentioned a man by the name of Mark Philips. Todd said that he was possibly the best detective in America, and he said that his son, Mark Philips, Jr., was turning out to be just as good. This man had to be Mark Philips, Jr. Sam noticed that, though Mark seemed to be relaxed, he was alert to his surroundings, and his right hand never moved far from his gun.

Sam turned to the other man. Tony seemed to be looking directly at Sam, but if there was any movement in the room, his eyes shifted slightly to take in the scene. Every muscle in his body was alert to any sign of danger. Several medals for bravery and honor decorated his uniform.

Next, Sam studied the café. The kitchen was in the back and the tables were arranged like a horseshoe. Tony and Mark sat where they could see both the front and back doors and every window. No one could sneak up on them, and they could make a prompt escape through either door.

Sam realized that he was sitting at a table with the two living, breathing, secret weapons of the railroad.

"I think, I understand," Sam said. "How long do you think it will take you to complete the job?"

Once again the two men looked at each other. This time it was Mark who spoke. "Like I said earlier, we really can't go into detail, but I think that it will not take long to find the perpetrators of these attacks on the railroad. It'll take no more than a couple of weeks, if everything goes as planned."

Sam sighed. He would have to continue to hide his secret from Esther. That would not be easy, but it could not be helped. "I guess I'll wait."

"We'll be leaving Miles City this afternoon, so chances are we won't be running into you or your family any time soon. That way they won't get suspicious about what's going on," Tony said.

"Good. Well, I'll be going." Sam rose to his feet. He gave both men directions to the ranch in case they needed him. It was arranged that

Mark would come and get Sam when Tony was done. Then they would decide what to do.

Sam knew that the next few days were going to be very hard. Esther would know that something was happening. As his horse carried him home, Sam wondered how he could continue to keep the news a secret. *Thank You dear Lord, for what we have found out*, he prayed. *Please continue to help us.*

"You mean it's true?" Tom exclaimed. Before going home, Sam had gone to see Tom, who was still building the fence.

"I think so," Sam said, smiling broadly.

"Yahoo! I bet Esther is thrilled! I can't wait to meet him! Is he at your house?" Tom prepared to mount his horse. He grabbed hold of the horn and swung his leg over the saddle.

"No, and I haven't told Esther yet."

Tom, half on and half off the horse, looked at his friend in astonishment and slid back down. "You haven't what?"

"I'll admit it sounds crazy, but I want to wait until I know for sure.

Tom was utterly confused. "I thought you did know for sure."

"No, I said I thought I know," Sam tried to explain. After telling Tom everything that had happened in town, he said, "I want to talk to Elmira Thornberry before I get Esther's hopes up. She grieves over the loss of Mac and Shane. If I tell her about Tony and then find out that he's not really her brother, it would simply crush her."

Tom nodded. "If that's the way you want it, Sam, she won't find out from me."

"Thanks, buddy."

A few hours before supper, Sam rode up to the hitching post.

Mike, sitting on the porch, waved to him. "Hi, Dad!" The boy jumped down and ran to meet him. "I'll take care of the horse for you," he offered.

"Thanks, Professor." Sam ruffled the boy's hair before handing him the reins.

"Sam, you're back!" Esther called. She ran out to greet him and he hugged her. "How did it go in town?"

Sam took a deep breath. "Come go for a walk with me, Esther honey." He took her hand and together they started toward a small meadow.

They were silent for a few minutes. Sam was trying to think of something to tell her that would ease her anxiety. *What can I say, Lord*?

he prayed. He smiled as he thought of a great explanation. *Thank You, Lord.*

"Esther, do you remember when we were on our honeymoon and you found that dress that you liked so well?"

She nodded.

"Do you remember when I left the house early one morning to get it, but I didn't tell you where I was going?"

She nodded again.

"'Member how you didn't question what I was doing? You knew that I must have had something very important to do."

She stopped walking and looked into his eyes. "Sam, what is it you're trying to tell me?"

"Esther, something big is happening. Something that may change our lives in such a wonderful way, but I'm not sure right now. We have to wait. After a while, a man and I may have to go on a trip. He has a job for the army that he has to complete first. When he's done, we'll probably leave. It'll take us a good bit of time, but I think the result will be worth it." He was running out of things to say. "You'll just have to trust me. Will you do that, Esther honey?"

Esther turned and surveyed their ranch. She watched her boys scampering around the yard in a game of tag. Duke was "it." He and the boys loved the game. When he chased them, sooner or later he managed to tackle one of them.

Esther looked back at Sam. "Sammy, I'll always trust you. Still, I want you to know that if it's money or riches, they don't mean a thing to me. I have the Lord, you, the boys, Carol and Tom, and that's what's important to me."

Sam grasped both of her hands. "Oh, Esther, it's something worth much more than money or earthly riches." He kissed her.

After dinner, Esther watched her husband tend to the evening chores with the boys trying to help. The younger ones were mainly getting in the way, but he was patient with them.

Esther remembered the twinkle in Sam's eye as he tried to explain a part of his secret to her. Esther had never seen that look before. *What could his secret be*? she wondered. *Lord, I don't understand what he's doing. I'm almost frightened that he's found some earthly treasure that has him captivated. Lord, please let him know that those things aren't important to me.*

Time seemed to drag for Sam. He tried to fill it with work. He and Tom finished the fence and continued tending crops and getting their ranch ready for stock. They stayed up all hours of the night figuring out the price of horses and cattle and the cost of feeding them. Still, Sam thought the days would never pass.

The Sunday after the meeting with Mark and Tony, Sam and Esther talked with Steve Kenneth after the morning service.

"Steve, have you heard how the railroad is doing?" Sam asked. His voice shook a little and he hoped no one noticed.

"Well, I know that they've been doing a lot of surveying, and so far the attacks have been few and far between. They must have some good men working on the problem." Sam suppressed a smile. Steve continued, "I've heard that if they get this project done no later than the end of this month, they plan to have the tracks laid all the way to Miles City by the end of the year. Of course that's their plan right now. It could take longer or it could get done sooner. It's hard, at this stage, to pin down the exact date."

"Oh, won't that be exciting?" Esther said. "Just think, Sam, we could get our herd next spring."

Sam smiled at her enthusiasm. He was blessed to have a wife who loved the things that he loved. "It sure is, Esther honey. One more question, Steve. Where can I go to get a couple of good cow ponies?"

"If you can wait until August, there'll be an auction. There's a large ranch in South Dakota that sends a herd of cowponies up here. They usually have a good selection of Mustangs and quarter-horses."

Jeff Ray joined them and said, "Those horses I use to pull my lumber wagons were bought from the auction. They are good horses."

"We can wait until then," Sam told them. "Thanks."

"You're welcome."

Chapter 8

The Pursuit Begins

Days went by and still no word from Tony. Sam could hardly stand the suspense. Finally, on May 20, around 6:00 P. M., Matt came running into the barn.

"Dad, there's a rider coming. I can't see who it is."

"I've never seen the horse before." Mac came in right behind his older brother.

Sam chuckled. In the short time that they had been at Miles City, Mac already knew just about every horse in the neighborhood.

After wiping his hands on a rag, Sam stepped out into the warm sunlight. He shielded his eyes and studied the approaching rider. His heart skipped a beat. It was Mark Philips.

"Howdy, Sam," he said as he trotted up to the barn.

"Hi, Mark." Sam reached up to shake his hand.

"We're through, and Tony said he's going to see the midwife. He wants to know if you're coming."

"I am."

"I'd like to go with you two, but I've got another job waiting for me. I wish you lots of luck though."

"Got the railroad business all squared away?"

Mark's countenance held a hint of pleasure. "All I can say is, the bad guys are locked up."

Sam had heard news of the arrests. A gang of outlaws had been trying to stop the railroad because the tracks were being laid near their hideout. He would never know how Tony and Mark alone had hunted them down and then finished the surveying job in record time.

Sam shook Mark's hand once again. "I hope we'll meet up again."

"Same here. Take care of my partner." Mark saluted, turned his horse eastward, and was gone.

Esther came out to stand by Sam.

"Who was that?"

"That was Mark Philips. He's been surveying for the railroad." Sam turned to look at her. "He came to tell me that my friend is ready. I need to leave as soon as possible."

Esther's face clouded. She reached for his hands. "Sam, I don't understand what's happening, but if you think you need to leave for a while, I'll not go against you. Just promise me you'll be very careful."

He leaned down to kiss her and whispered, "You have my word."

In less than an hour, Sam was ready. Tom and Carol rode in as he was tying his gear onto the saddle.

"Are you leaving, Sam?" Tom asked.

"Yeah."

"Leaving?" Carol echoed, looking first at Sam and then at Tom. "Where are you going?"

"A friend and I have some business we need to attend to." He looked at Esther and saw her brush away tears.

"Esther honey, please don't worry." He put his arms around her. "The Lord willing, when I come back I'll have some of the best news you have ever heard."

She looked up at him and forced a smile. "I'll miss you, Sammy."

"I'll miss you, Esther." Sam kissed her and then hugged each one of his boys.

"Are you sure I can't come with you, Dad?" Matt asked.

"There's no one I would rather have with me than you boys. I mean that, but I need you to stay here and take care of your mom and the ranch. Matthew, you're the man of the house while I'm gone. Okay?"

"Okay, Dad."

Sam jumped into the saddle and looked at Tom. "I feel bad leaving you here with all the work."

"Don't worry about it, Sam. I understand." Tom led them in prayer.

"Thanks, Tom. Bye everyone!"

Sam trotted out of the yard. Duke, sensing something was amiss, whined and pawed at Matthew's leg. The boy laid his hand on the dog's head. Esther put her arms around her two youngest sons and watched Sam ride away.

"Tom, do you know where he's going and what he's doing?" she asked softly.

"Yes, I do."

"You do?" Carol looked at him curiously.

"Can you tell me one thing?" Esther asked, turning to look at him. "Is it dangerous?"

Tom gave her an encouraging smile. "There's always the danger of travel, but his mission is not dangerous. Don't worry, Esther. If he's right, it'll definitely be worth the trip."

Esther turned back and gazed at the horse and rider who were quickly disappearing. *Lord, please keep him safe*, she prayed.

By the time Sam arrived in town, the last stage had already left. He and Tony got rooms at the hotel, and had a late supper. It was then that Sam learned Tony was also a Christian, having trusted Christ as his Saviour when he was nine.

At 6:00 the next morning, they boarded the stage.

"Well, Sam, here we go," Tony said, settling down in the seat. "Lord, please help us. Please help us to not only find the truth, but be able to witness to others along the way."

"Yes, Lord, please."

The stage could carry six people comfortably, three on one side and three on the other. On top of the stage was a rack for luggage. There was also a place for luggage on the back.

The driver sat on top, on a bench-like seat. Long lines gave him control of the horses. To his right was the brake. He had to keep his foot on it in case he had to stop. The mail and the moneybox, when there was one, rode beneath his seat.

The cargo and the path that they took often decided whether or not there was a man riding shotgun. His job was to sit by the driver and ward off anyone who might attack them.

On this trip, the stage was loaded to capacity, making private conversation impossible. Instead of discussing their plans, and since the other riders were not sociable, Sam and Tony pulled their hats down over their eyes and went to sleep.

The road was rough and the ride was long. Every ten miles the stage stopped at small makeshift stations where the passengers could stretch their legs and get something to drink. Every twenty miles, they changed horses.

Around noon they stopped, and a woman came out of the station to announce that lunch was ready.

"I'm starving," the man sitting across from Sam said. The six passengers climbed out of the stage and walked into the depot.

The food, such as it was, satisfied their hunger, and within an hour the stage was rolling again.

It was midnight when they pulled into the small town of Powderville, Montana. After Sam and Tony had removed their bags from the coach, they booked passage on the next stage to Hammond, Montana. It would be leaving at 6:00 the next morning. They each got a room and retired for the night.

"We got a man riding shotgun this time," Tony pointed out as they were waiting to get on the stage the next morning. "Wonder if we'll have any trouble."

When they boarded the stage, they found that they were sharing it with four new passengers.

"My name is Dan Knaplen," the man across from Tony said. "This is my wife, Randi. The lady next to her is her sister, Joetta Kain, and the gentleman across from her is—"

"Gerald Kain." The elderly, rather chubby man beside Sam quickly spoke for himself. "I'm the father of these two lovely ladies. I'm a businessman by trade. Out here, I have found that guns seem to be a necessity. So, I've chosen that particular piece of hardware as my main merchandise. If you need any type of weapon, I'll get it for you, and if I don't have it in stock, I'll send for it and charge you only half the price for your inconvenience, guaranteed."

The others laughed at his jolly manner. It was easy to like Gerald Kain.

"I'm Tony Glen."

"Sam Goodton." They exchanged handshakes and their journey started.

"Mr. Glen," Dan said, "I take it from your uniform that you're in the cavalry. Have you ever run into the bandit they call the Tumbleweed? I hear tell that the area we will be going through is where he hides out. Do you know if that's true?"

"His hideout is *rumored* to be here. However, there are no solid records of anyone ever seeing the man's face. So when people say they saw him and his gang, outside of a holdup, there's room for error."

"How do people know when it's Tumbleweed's gang that holds them up?" Sam asked.

"The man himself rarely rides on the holdups. His men have made it clear that their boss is back along the trail, out of sight, but keeping an eye on the robbery. Also, the men wear bandanas that have tumbleweeds on them, and they normally leave a piece of tumbleweed wherever they attack. To answer your first question, Mr. Knaplen, I myself have never tangled with him, but I heard of a detective who came very close to capturing him. He had the Tumbleweed cornered in a small town somewhere around here. In fact, he was walking up to the man to snap on the cuffs, but a couple of Tumbleweed's men came out of an alley and jumped him from behind. The bandit got away. He wore his hat low and turned up the collar of his jacket, so his face was never seen. However, the detective did see that the man had a fishhook-shaped scar on his right hand."

As the conversation drifted away from that subject, Sam asked Mr. Kain where he was going.

"It's indeed a long story," he said. "All four of us are originally from North Dakota, but three years ago a missionary named Andrew Fields came to our church. He is working in the little town of Putney, Wyoming. He stayed in our area raising support, and he and Joetta fell in love." He looked at his daughter and nodded for her to pick up the story.

"We stayed in contact by mail, and a year ago he proposed. He asked me to wait to join him until he could establish the work in Putney. Two months ago, he wrote and said that all was ready. At first, just father and I were going to go, but in Andrew's last letter, he said that he also wanted to build a hospital and a school."

"That's where we come in," Dan said. "I am a builder and my wife is a schoolteacher."

"So we all decided to come," Randi said with a smile.

"Some of my late wife's relatives live in Powderville, and we swung by there and saw them before traveling on down to Putney," Mr. Kain finished.

"That's wonderful," Sam said. "We will definitely keep you all in our prayers."

"Thank you," Kain replied.

The first ten miles of travel were past. The stage had left the station, and the passengers, refreshed by drinks of cool water, resumed their conversation. Dan was about to ask Sam why he was making this trip when the stage came to an unexpected halt. Tony, sitting next to the window, laid his hand on his gun. The three other men followed suit.

A lone man with a saddle slung over one shoulder and a saddlebag over the opposite arm was standing in the middle of the road.

"Pardon me," he addressed the driver. "Have you got room for one more? Lost my horse last night, and I've been walking a while. There's no town less'n ten miles from here. I was on my way to Hammond but decided to head back to Powderville to see if I could meet a stage."

"Well, we're pretty full, but maybe we can squeeze you in."

"Driver, perhaps I could be of some assistance," Mr. Kain said, climbing out of the stage. "If you don't mind, I'd enjoy a ride up top with you and your shotgun rider. You see, I used to drive a stage. Never quite got the thrill out of my system. This man is welcome to take my spot in the coach."

"You heard him, stranger." The driver smiled at the newcomer. "Come on."

"Thanks. Oh, by the way, which road are you folks taking to Hammond?"

"We planned on taking the new road," the driver answered.

"Good. It really don't matter to me, but that's the best way." The man lifted his saddle

to the shotgun rider. "I'll just hold the bags."
The shotgun rider nodded and secured the
saddle with the luggage.

"Do be careful, Father," Randi said as her
father prepared to climb to the top.

"I will, my dear," he promised. With his foot
on the wheel and his hand grasping the driver's
seat, he made his way up.

Tony grinned. "To be honest, I wasn't sure
if he could make it up there."

"Oh, my father's still pretty spry," Joetta
said with a smile.

Chapter 9

The Tumbleweed

Once the stage was rolling again, the passengers introduced themselves to the stranger.

"My name's George Kandle," the man said. "I'm on my way to Hammond to hook up with a friend of mine. He's bought a small herd of cattle and he's trying to start a ranch."

"I see," Tony said. "Um . . . when and where did you say you lost your horse?"

"Oh, I was about ten miles down the road making camp last night. A coyote spooked my horse. There was nothing I could do last night, so I went to sleep. Then this morning, I started out walking toward Powderville."

Tony had another question. "That's a mighty long walk, Kandle, but you say you got a full night's rest?"

"Sure did. I know this here trail like the back of my hand, and I know the best places to camp where I'll be safe. I can sleep outside with no problem."

Sam and Tony glanced at each other. The man was lying. They needed to warn the driver, but had to do it without making Kandle suspicious.

Lord, Sam prayed silently, *please help us.* He had barely finished praying when there was a snap and a loud thump.

"Whoa boys! Whoa!" the driver shouted to the team. As the horses came to a stop, Tony looked out the window to see what was going on.

"I'm sorry folks," the driver apologized. "One of the suitcases flew out of the back. I've never had that happen before."

Thank You, Lord, Sam exulted.

The suitcase was full of Mrs. Knaplen's schoolbooks. While she and her family were picking them up, Sam and Tony pulled the driver off to the side.

"That stranger's up to something," Tony whispered.

"How do you mean?"

"First he says he lost his horse ten miles down the road. Isn't it ten miles to the next station?" The driver nodded. "That's what I thought, and since it's the second stop, they have horses for the stage. If that man knows this country as well as he says he does, why didn't he stop at that station and borrow a horse, or at least wait for the stage to get there?"

"You've got a point," the driver said.

"And he claims to have walked ten miles in the amount of time that it took the stage to travel ten miles," Sam put in.

"That's right," Tony agreed. He glanced over at Kandle. "Look at his clothes. They're not dusty and sweaty, and he doesn't have a canteen. Hard to walk that far with no water."

The driver had another suspicion. "I wonder why he asked what way we were taking to Hammond. Even if he did somehow walk all that way, seems to me he'd be glad just to get a ride. I wouldn't be particular about which road the stage took."

"I think he wanted to find out so he could help someone ambush us. There must have been a code of some kind he and his friends used. Right now they may have already set themselves up on the new road."

"You might be right," the driver said with a sigh. He looked at Tony. "Soldier, we're carrying a lot of money on us, both in the mail and in the strong box. What're we going to do?"

Sam looked at his friend and prayed that God would give him wisdom.

Tony thought for a minute. "What about this old road?"

"It's not 'xactly *old*," the driver explained. "It's called that because the other road is brand new. You used to have to go around this area that's full of boulders. Now they've made a way right through it. Nothing wrong with the old road though. It's only about six miles longer."

"Is there a place for us to hole up if we do get attacked?" Tony asked.

The driver scratched his chin. "Come to think of it, there's a cave not too far off the road. Maybe only eight feet. As I recall, it always seemed deep enough for a stage to fit in, and if I remember correctly, there's a stream right by it. If someone had to hide and put up a fight, that'd be a grand spot."

"Let's take that road," Tony advised.

Soon they were all back in the stage.

Tony and Sam tried to act casual, but they were nervous. The others, not noticing, carried on a friendly conversation.

They had gone barely a mile when Kandle announced, "Here's the split-off. The old road goes left and the new one goes right."

The team turned down the old road.

"What's he doing?" Kandle yelled. "He's taking the old road! This ain't the right way! Stop him, stop him!" He reached for his gun, but both Tony and Sam had already drawn theirs. Kandle froze and Sam took his pistol.

"What's wrong, Kandle?" Tony asked. "I thought you said it didn't matter to you what road we took."

The man said nothing.

"Sam, look in his saddlebag."

Sam carefully took the bag from Kandle. He opened the flap and began to look though it.

"Look!" he exclaimed. He held up a green handkerchief decorated with tumbleweeds.

As the others gasped, Kandle tried to jump out of the stage, but Dan, who was sitting across from him, pulled the stage door shut. Sam grabbed Kandle's arm and held him.

"We need to tie him up," Sam said, looking back at Tony.

"Yeah, I know." Tony let the hammer down on his pistol. His coat was lying on the seat beside him. He reached under it and brought out a length of rope. "That's why I borrowed this from the driver."

"You think of everything don't you?" Sam praised.

"That's what I've been trained to do," he answered modestly.

Once the prisoner was secured, Tony holstered his pistol and finished looking through Kandle's saddlebag.

"Look what we have here. All kinds of stuff." Out of one side he pulled two fully loaded pistols, a map of the area, and some food. He lifted the flap to the other side. Out of the corner of his eye he saw Kandle flinch.

Inside the bag was a small pouch tied with a string. He opened it and nodded.

"That's what I thought. Looks like about a hundred dollars. Probably what Tumbleweed paid him to figure out which road we were taking."

Sorrow filled Joetta's countenance. "He was willing to put lives in jeopardy for one hundred dollars."

The stage had traveled two miles down the old road. No one spoke. Though they were going by a different route, Tumbleweed's gang could still attack them.

Sam and Tony, with Kandle bound and gagged between them, were keeping a sharp lookout. Suddenly, a bullet ricocheted off the side of the stage.

"Get down!" Tony fired in the general direction that the bullet had come from.

The stage lurched as the driver urged the horses into a dead run. Coming up behind the stage were ten riders.

Sam, Tony, and Dan emptied their pistols into the oncoming riders. Three pulled up wounded.

When Sam's pistol was empty, he went for the one in Kandle's pack.

"Here," Joetta said, reaching for the empty pistol.

"We can load," Randi added.

Dan, Tony, and Sam gave them their ammunition belts and empty guns. The ladies loaded them swiftly.

The stage gave another lurch, and for a minute the horses veered off the trail.

"What happened?" Dan shouted as he helped his wife regain her balance.

Tony listened for a moment but could no longer hear the shotgun being fired. "The driver must be hurt. The shotgun rider must have taken over."

Just then the horses sped up and the shotgun began blasting again.

"What's going on up there?" Tony asked, though no one "up there" could hear them.

"It's Father!" Joetta exclaimed. "He's driving the stage! Listen!"

True enough, the elderly gentleman had taken over for the wounded driver. The passengers could hear him encouraging the horses.

"Come on, ponies!" he shouted. "Come on now! Let's go! Come on!"

The stage was traveling faster than Tony or Sam had dreamed possible.

"What did your father-in-law do? Drive stages or race them?" Tony asked.

Dan was handing an empty pistol to his wife. He grinned, despite the bullets flying around them. "Probably a little of both."

"Hey, Tony, there's the cave," Sam said, relieved.

"Thank God," was his friend's reply.

Mr. Kain headed the horses toward the opening.

"Okay, Sam, the minute we're inside, you and I got to jump out and keep Tumbleweed's men from following us," Tony instructed.

"Right," Sam answered.

"Count me in, too," Dan said.

"We can sure use you. Get ready. Now!" Tony shouted.

The three men jumped out of the stage and took cover, all the while firing at the outlaws. The bandits quickly reined in and found shelter from the flying lead. Then all became silent.

Chapter 10

Blessings from a Bandit

Sam, sheltered by the protection of a rock, tried to calm his racing heart. His hand ached from gripping his pistol so tightly. Beside him was Dan, beads of perspiration trickling down his face. On the other side of the cave, Tony squinted as he searched the ground in front of him. Behind Sam, the stage sat at an angle in a cave barely deep enough to contain it. Sheltered behind it, the ladies were tending to the wounded driver. Kandle was there as well. Mr. Kain, armed with one of his pieces of "merchandise", was on top of the stage, using the luggage as cover. With him was the shotgun rider, who had introduced himself as Carter Grahams.

Dear Lord, Sam began to pray, *please help us.* He was scared, but the Lord reminded him of a time when Asa, king of Judah, was in a battle. Asa had prayed, "LORD, it is nothing with thee to help, whether with many, or with them that have no power: help us, O LORD our

God; for we rest on thee, and in thy name we go against this multitude. O LORD, thou art our God; let not man prevail against thee." Though the situation seemed hopeless, the assurance that the Lord was his strength gave Sam peace.

He heard a noise beside him and turned to see Dan praying. "Dear Lord, thank You that we made it to the cave and that the driver is not hurt badly. You are in control. Please help us. Amen."

"Amen," Sam echoed.

A few minutes later, both Sam and Dan jumped as Tony slid up next to them.

"Where'd you come from?" Sam asked.

"I came around the stage."

"I was so intent on watching out there that I didn't see you move," Dan said.

"I wanted to see if there's a back way out of this cave."

"Is there?" Sam asked.

Tony slowly shook his head. "Yes and no. At the back of the cave is an opening that leads straight up and out onto a ledge. But once you get up there, they'll have a clear shot. Here's my plan. You guys keep them busy and I'll crawl up there. If I can keep low, maybe they won't see me. I'll only be in the open for about four feet. I think there's enough cover for me to climb down. Once I'm down, I'll try to come up behind them and get the drop on them."

"All of them?" Dan asked.

"Yeah, there's only seven left, and I watched them as they took cover. They didn't spread out; they stayed together." Tony looked at Sam. "Well, what do you think?"

Sam prayed for wisdom. "There's no other way?"

"We could wait for help, but the driver said it might take days for a sheriff to find out we're missing. The only other way is to rush them, and obviously we don't want to do that."

The others agreed.

"Why don't you let me take the hard job, Tony?" Sam suggested.

"Two reasons. One, this was my idea. Two, you got a wife and children to take care of. Besides, I've done stuff like this before. So that makes three reasons. I'm the man to do it, but thanks though."

Sam looked at Dan, who nodded in agreement.

"Okay, Tony, but be careful," Sam cautioned.

"I will," he promised, and walked away.

Sam suddenly whispered, "Dan, I'll be right back." He jumped up and hurried into the cave. Tony had finished telling Mr. Kain and Grahams about his plan and was walking toward the opening. He had borrowed one of Mr. Kain's pistols and had it securely in his belt.

"Tony, Tony wait," Sam called softly as he approached him. "Let's pray before you go up."

When they were done, Tony said, "Thanks, Sam. Now, give me two minutes, then fire with everything you have."

"Right." Sam turned and ran back to Dan. "Dan, I'm going to the other side." By the time he was in position, two minutes had passed.

Lord, please help us. Keep Tony safe, he prayed. Laying his wrist on top of a flat stone for balance, Sam fired. At his signal, the others began to fire. The driver, his wound bandaged, was able to help with the diversion.

Once they had started firing, Tony began to make his way through the opening. He inched his head into the warm sunlight and when no bullets whistled by, he continued. In order to pull himself up out of the cave, he had to brace his feet against the sides of the opening and push on the ledge with his hands. The maneuver was difficult in the first place, but having to do it while staying low made it even harder. Finally, he was lying flat on the ledge.

On his stomach, he began to crawl to the right. When a bullet ricocheted off the ledge, Tony laid still. Apparently, it was a stray bullet, for no more came. *Thank You, Lord*, Tony prayed and continued to crawl. Soon he was across the flat rock. There was enough cover for him to make his way down the outside of the cave.

Meanwhile, the men in the cave kept firing. When one bandit attempted to get closer to the mouth of the cave, Sam fired and sent his pistol flying. The man yelped and dove for cover. Dan proved to be a good shot as well. When another outlaw swiftly leaned around a scrub for a better shot, Dan's bullet caught him in the wrist.

"Nice shot!" Sam shouted from across the cave.

"You too!" Dan shouted back. He ducked as a bullet hissed by him.

Tumbleweed's men aren't bad either, Sam thought when a bullet missed him by inches.

"Wonder where that soldier boy is," said Mr. Kain, still on top of the stage.

Grahams shrugged. He reloaded his weapon and clicked the barrel shut. "I think he must've made it," he said. He fired and the cave echoed the report.

Tony was getting into position. He had circled the outlaws and was coming up from behind. They were across the road from the cave, bunched together, using rocks and shrubs for cover. To their back was a large boulder with a second, larger one behind it, curving over it like a staff. A rock was wedged between them. From the front, the formation looked like a mouth with one tooth. Tony had crawled up into the "mouth" and was hiding behind the "tooth." He could see all seven of the outlaws, yet they could not see him.

After making sure both pistols were fully loaded, Tony fired at a tree in the center of their position.

"Hold it!" he shouted.

The seven men whirled around and looked for the shooter. Tony eased to the other side of the "tooth" and fired again.

"Drop your guns!"

Six of the men obeyed. The other slumped behind a rock and fired in Tony's direction.

"I wouldn't try that again!" Sam warned, coming up from behind. The outlaw scowled and curled his lip, but he let go of the weapon.

"You okay, Tony?" Sam called.

"Yep." He appeared from behind a clump of bushes to Sam's left.

Sam gave him a puzzled look. "I thought you were up there in that crevice."

"I was. I moved."

"When?"

"Just a minute ago."

Sam shrugged. "From now on I'll simply decide that you're not where I think you are; if you are there, you'll be moving soon. I can't keep track of you."

Dan, Grahams, and the driver came running up with some rope.

"Thanks." Tony reached for the rope. "Where's Mr. Kain?"

Grahams turned and looked back. "I thought he was right behind me. He climbed down off the stage right after I did."

"Here." Tony tossed the rope to Sam. "You, Mr. Shotgun, and driver, tie these men up. Come on, Dan. Let's go look for him."

When Tony and Dan had left, Sam looked at the driver. "How's the arm?"

"Not bad. I'll keep a gun on these hombres while you and Grahams tie them up. Oh, by the way, my name's Charlie Kolt and this is Carter Grahams." He smiled. "I guess this is kind of a funny time for introductions."

Sam grinned as he tied the first man up. "I'm Sam Goodton."

Tony and Dan could not find Mr. Kain. He was not in the cave and his two daughters had no idea where he was.

"Where could he have gone?" Dan asked, concerned.

Tony stepped out of the cave and began to search for footprints, but the ground was too rocky.

"Dear Lord, please let him be alright," Dan prayed aloud.

"Yes, Lord, please," Tony added. After searching outside the cave, they decided to walk back up the trail a bit. They had gone only about five yards when they heard a rustling in the woods. Tony pushed Dan behind him and drew his pistol.

"Don't shoot," a familiar voice spoke. "It's me."

"Mr. Kain?" Tony asked.

"Yeah! Look what I found." From out of the trees came four men, three of them wounded. Behind them walked Mr. Kain with his pistol pointed at them.

"Who are these guys?" Tony asked.

"Well, three of them are the ones you boys wounded. I'm not completely sure about the fourth one, but I remembered that you said the Tumbleweed never went with his men on raids, that he always hid back along the trail. So, while you boys were handling those outlaws, I went to see if I could find the leader. Found these three licking their wounds and this man watching through field glasses. Look at his right hand."

Tony looked and nodded in satisfaction. On the back of his hand was a scar shaped like a fishhook. Tony stepped back and began to chuckle.

"Mr. Kain, I think you've caught the Tumbleweed," he said.

The outlaw's face turned red. "Outsmarted by an old man," he growled.

With Mr. Kain driving the stage, they headed for Hammond. Tony, Sam, and the outlaws, some of them riding double, followed. At the next stop they borrowed more horses. Late that night they made it to Hammond.

The first thing they did was notify the sheriff. After telling him what had happened and handing the prisoners over to him, they retired for the night.

Early the next morning, Tony had a surprise for the Knaplens and Kains.

"Here, this is for you all," Tony said, handing Dan an envelope.

"What's this?" Dan asked. He opened it and his eyes widened in astonishment. "Why, there . . . there must be two thousand dollars here!"

"That's right. It's the reward money for the capture of the Tumbleweed and his men," Tony explained.

"But if anyone deserves this, it's you, Mr. Glen," Dan argued.

"No. I want you folks to have it, on one condition."

"What's that?" Dan asked.

"That you use some of it to help build a school and hospital."

Joetta's eyes filled with tears. "How can we ever thank you both?"

Randi smiled and took hold of her sister's hand. "Yes, how can we thank you?"

"Thank the Lord," Tony said.

Dan nodded and began to chuckle. "Who would have ever thought God could use a bandit to bring a blessing like this."

Chapter 11

A Thorough Search

The stage had to be patched up and a new driver sent for from a neighboring ranch where he worked when not driving a stage. There was a small church in town, and Tony and Sam attended it. The next day they traveled to Alzada, Montana, from there to St. Onge, South Dakota, and on to Rapid City.

"Well, Sam," Tony began, as they walked up the steps to their hotel rooms. "We're about a third of the way there."

"Don't remind me," Sam teased. "I'm ready to settle back down to some relaxing ranch work."

Tony laughed, but when he stopped in front of the door to his room, he became serious. "If this turns out to be a wild goose chase, it will still be worth it just to have been able to help the Knaplens and Kains."

Sam nodded. "Yep, you're right."

It took seven more days of hard travel from Rapid City through Wall, Belvidere, Vivian, Chamberlain, Plankinton, and Emery to reach Sioux Falls, South Dakota. By then they had been on the road for thirteen long days. It was a relief to know the train would take them to their final destination in one day.

Sam missed Esther terribly. Every time he found a telegraph office, he sent her a note telling her he was all right, that he loved her and missed her.

The train arrived in Minneapolis late in the evening on June 3.

"Sam, we're here," Tony said as the train slowed down and awoke him.

"Oh, praise the Lord," Sam said, pushing his hat back from his eyes.

They stood and grabbed their bags from the rack above them. When it was their turn, they stepped off the train.

"Wow," Sam said in awe. Even at night the city was amazing. Bright lights radiated from many of the buildings. Some of the structures were taller than any Sam had ever seen.

"Yeah, it's a pretty big place." Tony looked about. "Hey look, there's a hotel. Come on.

We can start looking for Mrs. Thornberry tomorrow."

"Sounds good to me," Sam said, stifling a yawn. "I'm tired."

The hotel was a fancy one. Sam and Tony, disheveled and dusty from their long trip, received several disdainful glances from the more refined guests.

"If I were you," Tony whispered to Sam, "I'd wear the best you have tomorrow. Else we might not be greeted too friendly around here."

"You're not kidding."

When they met outside their rooms the next morning, they looked at one another in surprise.

"Boy, do you look different," Sam chuckled. Tony had traded his dusty uniform for his dress uniform, shaved his two-week-old beard, and polished his boots until they glistened.

Tony locked the door behind him. "I might add that you don't look the same as you did last night, either."

Sam smiled as he looked down at his clothes. He wore an older but nice Sunday-go-to-meeting suit. With his bright red hair neatly combed and his boots cleaned, he looked pretty good.

"First thing to do is pray for help," Tony said.

"No argument there."

"Dear Lord, if it be Thy will, please help us to find Mrs. Thornberry. I pray that she will tell us the truth. Please guide us to the right places and keep us safe. I also pray for the friends we have made on this journey, and I pray for Sam's family, that You would keep them safe. Thank You, dear Lord, for being with us. In Your name we pray. Amen."

"Amen," Sam repeated. "Now what?"

"We start asking people. First stop, the hotel manager."

The manager, a middle-aged man who they found was also a deacon, was sorting mail behind the desk.

"Excuse me, sir," Tony began.

"What can I do for you? I do hope your rooms are to your liking."

"Oh yes, very much. We're trying to find an old acquaintance of mine. Her name is Thornberry, Elmira Thornberry."

"Thornberry . . . The name doesn't ring a bell. Let me do a quick check of my logs." It took him ten minutes to search his records.

"Sorry, gents, but no one by that name has ever stayed here."

"Thanks anyway," Tony said.

"I'd try the police station," the man called out as they left the hotel. "It's three blocks down and three blocks over."

"Much obliged."

Outside, Sam once again gazed at the splendor around him.

"How I wish Esther could be here with me. She would love all this."

They were passing a dress shop when Sam stopped. Inside was a beautiful pale green shawl trimmed with white lace.

Tony took several steps before he noticed that Sam was no longer with him. He walked back to where Sam was standing.

"What's up?"

"Do we have time for a small detour?"

Tony followed his friend's gaze. "I think so."

Sam stepped into the store. Through the window, Tony watched him purchase the shawl and give instructions to have it sent to their hotel. Though he could not hear their conversation, Tony could tell Sam was asking about Mrs. Thornberry. The lady behind the counter shook her head. Sam thanked her and walked out.

"Thanks," he said to Tony. "That saleslady is a Christian. She made us a list of the churches in town and suggested that we check with the pastors."

On their way to the police station, they enquired about Mrs. Thornberry at two churches, a hospital, and a school. The answer was always the same. Even the police station could offer no immediate help.

"We have no records of her here," the elderly officer said, "but you see, we work only the south side of the city. There's another station up on the north side of town. I'd try there."

After getting directions, they left.

"I don't know about you, but I've got a headache," Sam said, rubbing his forehead.

"I'm just hungry. Come on, let's see if we can find a place to eat that won't exhaust our money supply."

It took some doing, but they finally found a restaurant with tasty food at a reasonable price.

"That was good," Tony said with a satisfied sigh. He pushed back his plate and closed his eyes.

"Yeah." Sam finished the last of his coffee. "Praise the Lord, my headache's gone."

"Good," Tony responded sleepily. "Well, Sam, we're never going to find her sitting here." Wearily, he stood up.

They reached the north police station around 4:00 that afternoon. Sam and Tony asked the young sergeant, who was also a Sunday School teacher, about the midwife.

"Let me check our files." He went to a tall cabinet and opened the next to the last drawer. There was a rustle of paper as he looked for the letter *T*.

"Here's the *T*'s. Let's see. "Thornberry . . . T-H . . . T-H-A . . . T-H-E . . . T-H-I . . . T-H-O. . ." On he went until he smiled broadly. "Here we go. Thornberry." He pulled out a folder and laid it on his desk.

Sam and Tony, their hearts racing, crowded close.

"What was that first name again?"

"Elmira," Sam and Tony answered.

"Here's a Randolph and Elmira Thornberry."

"That's them," Tony nearly shouted.

"Okay." The sergeant wrote down the address. "Here you are."

"Thank you, sir, thank you very much," Tony said.

"Yes, thank you," Sam added.

They left the station and looked at the address.

"It looks like it's a ways away," Tony said.

"Yeah, by the time we get there it'll be late. What say we catch a cab home and go talk to her in the morning?"

Tony wanted to go see her then, but knowing Sam's decision was best, he shoved the paper in his pocket, found a horse-drawn cab, and they stepped on board.

"Where to gentlemen?" the driver asked from the raised seat behind them.

"The Minneapolis Hotel," Tony instructed.

"Right," the driver said. Using long lines to control the horse, he urged it into its customary clip.

On the way to the hotel, Tony pulled the slip of paper out of his pocket and studied it. Sam noticed that he appeared disturbed.

"What's wrong?"

His friend began nervously. "Sam . . .

I'm . . . afraid that maybe none of what we think is true. It could be that Shane Maker wasn't the only boy Mrs. Thornberry delivered on that day."

"You could be right, but remember, God's in control. If we're wrong, He still has a reason for all this."

"I know and I sure am glad."

Chapter 12

Elmira's Secret

After breakfast the next morning, Sam and Tony set off for the midwife's house. It took them forty minutes to get there by a horse-drawn cab.

The cabby opened the door. "Here we are, sirs. God bless you."

"Much obliged," Sam said, dropping money into his hand.

As the cab drove off, they gazed at the house in front of them. Sam could see Tony was nervous. He laid his hand on Tony's shoulder and began to pray.

"Lord, You've led us to this place. Please help us on this last step to finding the truth. Thank You, Lord. Amen."

They walked to the door and Tony knocked. When a gray-haired lady answered, Tony removed his hat.

"Mrs. Elmira Thornberry?"

"Yes, who might you be, sonny?"

"I'm Tony Glen."

The woman's face lit up and she opened the door wide. "Oh . . . oh my," she said, taking hold of his hands. "Yes, yes, I see now. My how you've grown. Come in and sit yourself down." She led him to a long couch and sat down beside him, her eyes never leaving him.

"I was just thinking of you the other day," she said. "I still have the pictures and all the little notes you sent me. Oh, how I've missed your letters, my boy. Tell me, how are your parents?"

Tony's smiled faded. "Well, they both have passed on."

"Oh, my poor boy," she said tenderly. "I'm sorry." She turned to brush away her tears, and it was only then that she saw Sam.

"Oh, pardon me, sir." She turned to face Tony. "Is this a friend of yours?"

"Yes, this is Samuel Goodton."

"Howdy, ma'am," Sam said, nodding to her.

"Hello, here, allow me to take your hats and coats." She quickly gathered them and laid them over a small table before coming back to Tony's side.

"I can't believe you're here. I remember when your mother wrote and said that you'd joined the army. I was so proud. How I wanted to see my boy in his uniform, and now you're here. Oh, but enough of my chatter. Please tell me why you came."

Tony prayed silently before saying, "Aunt Elmira, I've come to find out who my real parents were."

She smiled in a motherly way. "I figured. Son, I can't tell you. It's a secret; they asked me never to tell anyone."

"Aunt Elmira, Sam's wife's maiden name is Maker."

The woman caught her breath but quickly recovered. "Should that mean anything?"

"The Makers lived where Dad and Mom used to live. They had a son born on the same day that I was born, and you delivered us both."

"Oh, Tony, I delivered sometimes ten babies in one day. That means nothing."

"What *does* mean something is that they had a baby die mysteriously a few days after birth. It was only after that baby died that you gave me to the Glens. Why didn't you give me away the day I was born if my real parents didn't want me? Why did you wait?"

"Tony, there are things you don't understand."

"What things?" he asked gently. "All I want is the truth."

"You've been told a thousand times." She rose from her seat and was about to tell him not to bring it up again when an elderly man rolled into the room in a wheelchair.

"Tell him the truth, Elmira."

"What do you mean?" she asked, tears streaming down her cheeks.

"I don't know what happened with Tony Glen and the Maker's baby, but I know there's more to the story than what you've told everyone. It's bothered you all these years. Now's your chance to tell the truth."

Tony went to her side. "Aunt Elmira, I'm not here to cause you or Uncle Randolph any trouble. I only want to know what really happened. Please, Aunt Elly."

She looked into Tony's pleading eyes and sighed. She sat back down on the couch and Tony sat beside her. To reassure her, he held one hand and Uncle Randolph held the other. Sam leaned forward.

"I'll never forget that day." She seemed to choke on the words. "Early that morning, Lisa

Maker went into labor. She had already lost one son, and so we were all excited about this new baby. Mr. Maker had gone for the doctor in case there were complications. I had been with them for a week to help in any way I could. Soon the doctor was there, and he was just in time. The baby was on his way. Everything was going well, but then things went wrong. The chord was wrapped around the baby's neck, and he was choking. There was nothing I could do, because the doctor was trying to help the baby. I . . . I went to Lisa's side and grasped her hand. I remember how tightly she squeezed. She was trying so hard to have that baby. It seemed like such a long, long time. Finally the baby came, but Lisa was dying. The strain was too much on her. The doctor handed me the baby and said, 'Take care of him.' He went to help Lisa, but I knew, or I thought, it was too late for her. I . . . I took the baby." She paused and looked at Tony. "I took *you*, Tony, and began to care for you in another room. I wrapped you in a blanket, and when you began to cry, I held you close and rocked you. I had delivered many babies before you, but you did something no other baby had ever done. You looked up at me and smiled, and my heart melted. I thought that your mother would die and your father would put you in an orphanage. I don't know why I thought that. I should've known better but . . . I couldn't bear the thought of you growing up without parents who loved you. I began trying to find a way to help you. Lisa didn't get better that night, so I took you home with me like the doctor said.

"The next day and the next showed no sign of improvement in Mrs. Maker. In fact, she was doing worse. So, I took you to the Glens. I . . . they . . . it . . . it was all so mixed up. I was going to wait until Lisa died, but the Glens were moving the next day. I had to hurry. So I gave you to them and told them that your parents didn't want you. The Glens were thrilled at the thought of having a son, and they never asked any questions. They trusted me. Don't blame them, Tony. I planned to tell your real dad after your mom died, but . . . but suddenly she started getting better. Then in two weeks, she was well enough to care for the child. I should've told them the truth, but I was afraid. My nephew was a coroner, so I asked him for a burial certificate. I lied to him, too, and he gave me what I wanted. I took a small box, filled it with dirt, and buried it in the cemetery. Then I told the Makers that you had died. Oh Tony," she cried, "can you ever forgive me?"

Elmira Thornberry wept quietly. Tony was silent, trying to adjust to the idea that he had a new family that loved him. Sam smiled, rejoicing that his new friend was Shane Maker. Mr. Thornberry continued to hold his wife's hand, relieved that she had finally told the truth.

When he found his voice, Tony said, "I forgive you, Aunt Elly." He pulled the old woman close in a loving embrace. She clung to him.

"God be praised," Uncle Randolph whispered.

"I'm a Christian," Elmira said. "I knew that what I was doing was wrong. God was telling me not to do it, but I wouldn't listen. I thought I knew better than God. Ever since then, I've never been able to enjoy a service at church. I get no pleasure in reading my Bible. I knew it was because of what I had done. Now I have such peace that I've told the truth. How I wish I had done it sooner. I still have to talk to the Makers."

Sam spoke up. "Mrs. Thornberry, I know the Makers well. I would prefer that you let me tell them. I know that they have already forgiven you, but if you want to write them a letter, I will deliver it."

"Oh, thank you, young man. I'll do that."

Sam and Tony stayed there the rest of the day. After supper, they left with the promise of attending church with the Thornberrys the next day.

Most of the way home, Tony stared quietly out the window of the cab. Sam, too, was quiet. The news was overwhelming enough to him. He wondered how Tony felt.

"I can't believe it," Tony said, breaking the silence. He turned to look at Sam, and Sam saw tears flowing down his face. "Dad died first. Then a year later, Mom died, and I felt alone. I mean, I knew God was with me, and that comforted me, but I missed my parents. I thought about looking for my real family, but that seemed hopeless. And besides, I thought they didn't want anything to do with me. Then I met Mark. He and I became best friends, and he shared his family with me in every way he could. I was thankful for that, but I still felt kind of lonely. God was so good to me, and He helped me draw close to Him through that time." He paused and swallowed hard. "You have no idea what this feels like. To know that there's a family out there that I belong to!" He smiled. "I have a mom and a dad, a sister, a brother-in-law, and five nephews! I . . . I can't believe it. It seems too good to be true! I want to know everything about them—where they live, what they're like, what things they like, where you met them, how you proposed to my sister, and anything else you can think of!" His face beamed with joy.

Sam chuckled and held up his hands. "Whoa, one question at a time. Besides we're at the hotel."

Tony opened the door and jumped out. "I guess it'll have to wait, but I don't know if I can stand it. I'll never sleep tonight."

Chapter 13

To Meet the Makers

They were ready early the next morning and went to church with the Thornberrys. After the service, they all had Sunday dinner with the pastor and his wife.

That night after church Sam said, "We have to talk."

"No kidding. Come on. Let's go get a cup of coffee."

After the waitress had brought coffee, Sam spoke the question that was on his mind. "What do we do now?"

"Let's pray," Tony said. After prayer, he lifted his head and looked at Sam. "What do you think we should do?"

"Go to Indiana and tell the Makers. We're already this close, and we can make it there in one day by train. Then, we'll do whatever they want to do."

Tony nodded. "That sounds good to me."

Monday morning found Tony and Sam on the train to Clear Water.

"So," Tony said as the train began to roll.

Sam knew what Tony wanted. He started as far back as he could remember. He told about the time his mother was sick while she was pregnant with Sam's brother, and about how the doctor, after tending to her, informed her that Esther had fallen off the barn roof and broken her arm. He told about the Greys adopting the Indian girls and how Esther had befriended them. He went into great detail describing the Makers' personalities. He talked about beginning to court Esther; about how nervous he was when he first talked to her dad, and recounted the times he had spent with Esther, Carol Grey, Tom, and their chaperones. He told of asking Esther's dad permission to marry her and about proposing to her. He told about making the announcement at church that night, only to find that Tom and Carol were engaged as well.

He told about his own life, about his boys, and about Tyler coming home. He told about the lives of Tom and Carol. After recounting their wedding, he told about finding that Tom and he were related. Soon, he was telling about their trip west and their lives once they got there.

"Now," he said, "this is the most important part." He told about how he, Carol, and Tom had accepted Christ as their Savior. He finished with Esther's testimony.

"She was eight years old. That Christmas eve her mother told her about the death of her two older brothers. Esther couldn't believe it. She asked her why God would take them from their family. Mrs. Maker told her that God had a reason and that she had decided to trust in His wisdom. Esther left the room upset but, after thinking over what she had learned, realized that her mother was not angry. Instead, she was serving God faithfully.

"Esther went back and asked her how she could still love God. Mrs. Maker explained that God loved her and would only do what was best for her. She told Esther that since God cared enough to die for her and save her, she could trust Him. She said that once you get saved, God helps you get through all the trials of life. That was hard for an unsaved little girl to understand, but Esther knew that she wanted to have peace like her mom had. She knew the only way to get it was to ask Jesus to save her. She already knew that she was a sinner and that death was the penalty for sin.

She knew that to get saved she had to admit to God that she was a sinner and ask Him to save her. So she told her mom that she wanted to get saved.

"Mrs. Maker took her Bible and showed her Isaiah 53:6. 'All we like sheep have gone astray; we have turned every one to his own way; and the LORD hath laid on him the iniquity of us all.' She explained that if Esther would recognize that she was a sinner, a sheep gone astray, and put her trust in what Jesus did on Calvary after her sin had been laid on Him, she could be saved. That night, Christmas Eve, Esther became a child of God."

Sam paused and smiled at Tony, who had tears in his eyes.

"So, though you weren't there, you had a part in Esther's salvation."

"God is good," Tony said. "Not only did I get a new family, I'm blessed that they are Christians. Thanks for telling me all this, Sam. I wanted to know everything when we started, but I was afraid that maybe we were wrong and I really had no right to know. Now, I can't hear enough about my family." He paused. *"My family. I can't wait to meet them."*

They arrived at Clear Water that evening. After Sam left his hometown to head west, the little train station was replaced with a much larger one. Its size was proof of how much Clear Water had grown. Tony and Sam rented horses and rode out to Sam's parents' house. They had decided to spend the night there and go see the Makers the next morning.

Joshua and Mary were overjoyed to see their son. They were even more thrilled when they learned the reason for the visit.

"Welcome, Tony, welcome," Joshua said, shaking Tony's hand warmly.

"Yes, welcome," Mary echoed. "Sam, you take your old room and Tony can have Tyler's room."

Tony retired right away to give Sam time with his parents. They spent half the night talking about things that had happened since Sam left.

Mary fixed a bountiful breakfast the next morning.

"That was good, Mom," Sam said. He had eaten four pancakes, five sausages, and a second helping of ham and eggs. "I love you."

Soon they were on their way to the Makers' house. Sam was unsure about how to explain the situation. He knew that no matter what he said, they would be thrilled, but he still wanted to do it right. "Please help me, Lord," he whispered when the house came into view.

Tony stopped and waited out of sight. As Sam rode into the yard, Mr. and Mrs. Maker stepped out on the porch. "Sam!" they cried and ran to meet him.

He greeted them and quickly assured them that Esther and the boys were well.

"I came," he said slowly, "to deliver this letter to you. Don't worry, it's really good news."

There on the porch, Mr. and Mrs. Maker read Elmira's letter and they began to weep. The letter ended with, *"I'm so sorry. I wish there was something I could do to make up for the wrong that I've done. Enclosed is my address. If you wish to press charges, I understand."*

Mr. Maker looked up at Sam. "Sam," he said in a hoarse whisper, "is . . . is all this true? Is our boy really alive and well?"

"Yes, sir, he is." Sam turned back to where Tony was waiting. Sam waved to him and Tony trotted into the yard.

He dismounted and stood before his parents. Sam was not sure who moved first, but suddenly they were in each other's arms hugging and crying.

"Oh, praise God!" Mr. Maker cried. "Glory be to Thy Holy name!" He saw Sam quietly walk back to his horse and he said, his voice deep with emotion, "Thank you, Sam."

Sam grinned. "You're welcome, but it was all the Lord. Can I tell everyone I meet today?"

"Oh, please do," Mrs. Maker said tearfully. "Please do."

He turned his horse and rode away. He spent the rest of the day visiting. His first stop was Tyler's house. He met little Archibald Samuel, who was born after Sam left for Montana. Tyler and his family were thrilled by the news about Shane.

Tyler was the manager of his father-in-law's business in Clear Water and was thinking of starting another branch in Indianapolis. He and Cecilia loved the work, and Sam was happy for them.

As the evening drew to a close, Sam rejoiced at having seen family and friends. The news about Shane Maker spread quickly.

Everyone wanted to meet him, but would wait until the Makers were ready.

When Sam arrived back at the Makers, he found them in the living room.

"Come in, Sam," Lisa invited.

Tony was between his parents on the sofa. Sam had never seen Laramie and Lisa so happy.

"Shane—I mean—Tony tells us that Esther doesn't know about this," Mr. Maker said. "He explained why you didn't tell her. I believe that was wise. Thank you, Sam, for caring for her so."

Sam was too moved to reply. He missed Esther terribly.

"Dad?" Tony hesitated. Calling them Mom and Dad brought a rush of emotion.

Mr. Maker beamed at the title. "Yes, my son."

"I've been thinking about my name. I'm Shane Maker, but I'm also Tony Glen. So, I've been thinking that we need to somehow put them all together. What do you think of this? Shane first, because I was born with that name. Tony for the middle name, because that's what my adopted parents named me and that's what so many people know me by. For the last name . . ." He paused. If he went with Maker, the name of the family that reared him would be forgotten, but staying with Glen would be like turning his back on his real family.

The Makers realized his dilemma and Lisa took his hand.

"Son, whatever you decide will be fine with us. We can't ask you to give up the name you've known all your life. If you want to stay with Tony Glen, that's fine."

"Yes, it is," Laramie assured him.

Tony smiled his thanks.

"Why don't you use both last names?" Sam asked.

"There's a thought," Shane said. "Shane Tony Glenmaker."

"Oh, I like it!" Lisa exclaimed.

"So do I," Laramie agreed.

"Shane Tony Glenmaker," Shane repeated. "It's perfect. Praise the Lord."

Sam, his heart full, looked down at the table and saw a letter that the three Makers had started. It was to Mrs. Thornberry. Sam's smile widened as he read, *"We're sorry for being angry at you. Please forgive us. We forgive you."*

Chapter 14

Home!

The church at Clear Water held a Wednesday morning service the next day, so that Sam could be there when everyone was introduced to Shane. Sam enjoyed attending the church where he grew up and hearing his friend Terry Carson preach. Right after the service, Sam headed home to tell Esther the good news. After Shane had spent some time with his parents, he would follow.

Sam found his seat in the crowded train car. Looking back over the events of the past few weeks, he recalled the day he first met Mark. *All this started because Esther ran out of flour*, he thought to himself. *God had let that happen at just the right time. Lord, only You could have worked all this out. I'm so thankful for what You have done.* He thought of Deuteronomy 3:24. "O Lord GOD, thou hast begun to shew thy servant thy greatness, and thy mighty hand: for what God is there in heaven or in earth, that can do according to thy works, and according to thy might?"

On June 22, Sam's stage pulled into Miles City. Scott McBride was waiting at the station to pick up a package. "Sam!" he exclaimed as his friend got off the stage.

"Howdy, Pastor," Sam shook his hand. "Did Tom tell you why I had to leave?"

"Yes, he did. What did you find out?"

Sam smiled. "That man is my wife's brother."

"Well, praise the Lord! What a blessing! I'll be looking forward to hearing the whole story."

"Thank you, Pastor." Sam picked up his bags and walked to the livery stable. He rented a horse and headed home.

The sun was setting when Sam saw his ranch. Joy welled up inside him as he urged the horse into a canter.

Esther was finishing the dishes when she heard hoofbeats and Duke's bark. It was the special bark that meant he liked whoever was coming. She ran to the window.

"Sam!" She dropped the towel, flung open the door, and ran to him.

Sam jumped from his horse and wrapped his arms around her.

"Oh, Sam, I missed you so much," she cried, clinging to him.

Sam kissed her. "I missed you my darling. Esther honey," he whispered, "I'm sorry I had to leave, but when you hear why you'll understand."

"Daddy!" The boys were running across the yard toward them. Esther stepped back to let them greet their father.

"My boys, my boys," Sam said as they crowded around him. After hugs, all five began talking at once.

"Did you find what you were looking for?" asked Matthew.

"Where'd you go?" asked Mike.

"Was it exciting?" adventurous Mac wanted to know.

"Did you go with a soldier?" asked Montana.

"Did you find a treasure?" asked Martin.

Duke chimed in, barking so loudly that he threatened to deafen everyone.

"Whoa, whoa, slow down," Sam begged, still in a half-sitting, half-kneeling position. "I promise to tell you all about it soon, but first I have to talk to your mother. You've been patient a long time, and I'm proud of you. Do you think you could wait about twenty more minutes?"

"Sure we can, Dad," Matthew said. "Come on, guys, let's let Mom and Dad talk." The older brother led the other four boys into the house.

Sam stood and took Esther's hand. Together, they sat on the porch. Duke, happy that his master was home, lay down at Sam's feet. His tail thumped the ground.

"Okay, here's the story," Sam began, as Esther leaned against him. "The day I went into town to get you flour, I met this man. A few days later he introduced me to his friend. This friend was adopted when he was only a couple of days old. The midwife that delivered him said that his real parents didn't want him and that they had asked her to find him a good home."

"Oh, how sad," Esther murmured.

"Yes. Now he is grown and is in the army. Several years ago his adopted parents died, leaving him without a family. I thought that I might know who his real family was. So he and I went to Minneapolis to find the midwife."

Esther drew back and turned to look at him. "You went all the way to Minnesota?"

"Yes, and praise the Lord, we found her." Without mentioning names, Sam told the midwife's story.

"That's both wonderful and heartbreaking. To think that his mom and dad have thought he was dead all these years, and that he thought his real parents didn't want him. Were you able to find his real parents?"

"Yes." Sam took a deep breath. "Esther honey, the man's adopted name is Tony Glen, but his real name is—Shane Maker."

Esther's hand went to her heart. For a moment she looked at Sam in astonishment. "What . . . what did you say?" she asked shakily.

"Shane didn't die, Esther."

"You . . . you mean that . . . that my brother is . . . is alive?"

Sam nodded.

Esther sat there a moment, and then began to tremble. Sam took her in his arms.

"Sam, oh Sam, I . . . I . . . it . . . oh, Sam," she wept.

Sam held her tighter. "I know darling, I know."

"God is so good."

"Yes, yes He is."

Esther sat up and began wiping her eyes. "Where is he now?"

"He's with your mom and dad. We went to Clear Water after we talked to Mrs. Thornberry. We decided to let him stay there and get to know them while I came back to tell you. He should be coming sometime early next month."

"Mom and Dad must be so overjoyed," Esther said, a radiant smile on her face.

"They sure are, and Shane is just as pleased. Wait until you meet him, Esther honey. He looks like your dad, and you can tell that you and him are brother and sister. Oh, and Montana looks more like him than you could ever imagine."

"Is he . . .?" Esther began.

"Yes, Esther, he's saved."

"That makes it even more special." She sighed contentedly. "Praise the Lord. You were right, Sam. This does change our lives in such a wonderful way. Thank you."

"The Lord worked it all out, Esther. I'm thankful I got to get in on it. We—" Sam heard movement in the house and he chuckled. "I better go tell the boys what's happened or they might explode with curiosity."

"Sam, do you mind if I stay out here?"

He understood and touched her face gently. "I don't mind." He gave her a kiss before stepping into the house.

Esther sat on the porch and let her eyes sweep over the sights around her. How blessed she was. *Thank You Lord for keeping my Sam safe, and thank You that this had nothing to do with earthly treasures,* she prayed.

Later that evening Sam gave Esther the shawl he had bought in Minneapolis.

"Sam, it's beautiful! Thank you."

"You're welcome, Esther honey." He took her hand. "Thank *you,* darling, for trusting me."

Chapter 15

Uncle Shane

Esther spent the following days cleaning her house. She wanted everything to be as perfect as possible for her brother's arrival. The boys, thrilled to find out that they had another uncle, helped with anything she needed. Carol pitched in, too. Tom and Sam worked hard trying to get work done at the ranch so that there would be time to spend with the new member of the family.

On July 5, a man rode into the Silver Arrow ranch. Sam and Tom had just come back from the field and were putting their horses in the corral.

Tom saw him first. "Sam," he whispered. "Is that him?"

Sam turned and followed Tom's gaze. He squinted, trying to identify the rider coming down the hill toward the house. He smiled. "Yeah, yeah, Tom, it is!" He ran to the house and threw open the door. "Esther, Esther honey, he's here! Come quick!"

Esther, Carol, and the boys rushed outside.

Shane was only a couple of yards from the house. Sam took Esther's hand and helped her down the porch steps.

Shane came to a halt in front of them and dismounted. Sam stepped forward and shook his hand. "Good to see you again, Shane."

"Same here."

Sam turned to Esther. "Shane, this is your sister Esther. Esther, this is Shane."

The others backed away to let them greet each other. Shane tipped his hat to her. Esther, trying hard to keep from crying, smiled back. Both spoke at once. They chuckled nervously and Shane said, "You first."

"I'm so glad to meet you," she told him.

"Me, too. I've wanted a brother and a sister for as long as I can remember. Now I find that I've got a brother in Heaven and a sister on earth."

Sam could not tell who moved first, but Shane and Esther ended in an embrace. Sam, Tom, and Carol watched with tears in their eyes.

When they stepped away from each other, Sam introduced the rest of the crowd, and they went into the house.

The boys took an instant liking to Shane and he to them. He spent half the night telling them stories about the army. They sat close to him, absorbing every word.

When Shane had finished his last story of the night, Montana spoke up. "I'm gonna be a soldier."

"Are you?" Shane asked. The boy nodded.

"Say 'yes sir'," Sam corrected.

"Yes, sir," Monty said. "When I get big, I'll be a soldier."

"All soldiers have a curfew," Esther said, "and it's past yours, boys. Now, say goodnight to Uncle Shane." The name Uncle Shane brought a tear to her eye. She looked up at her brother and smiled.

"You heard your mother," Sam said. "Come on, I'll help you. The first one in bed gets to hear the bed-time story first."

The boys said goodnight and Sam followed them upstairs.

"Esther, if you don't mind, Tommy and I will go home," Carol said.

"Yeah, it's past our curfew, too," Tom added.

After Tom and Carol had gone, Esther and Shane began to talk. He told her about his life and she told him about hers. Shane had already heard many of the things she told him, but he doubted that the stories would ever grow old to him.

Both of them had many questions to ask each other.

"Has Monty always wanted to be a soldier?"

"I've called him 'Little Soldier' since he was a baby, but a couple of months ago was the first time *he* said he wanted to be a soldier. Why did you join the cavalry?"

"My dad was a soldier, a sergeant. So were his dad, his grandfather, and his great-grandfather. Four generations of soldiers. Dad wanted me to be the fifth one, but he told me that if I decided not to, it would be fine with him. He wanted me to do what God wanted. I was sure that I'd never join the army, but right after I turned eighteen, a man who had escaped from the army prison shot my dad. Even with a bullet in his arm, Dad caught the man before he made it to the fort gate. I saw dedication in my father. He loved the army.

So I really began to pray about what God wanted. I was reading my Bible and read about Joshua. Man, what a soldier. After reading about him, I knew that God wanted me to join the army. I've never regretted it."

Duke, having seen the boys safely to bed, made his way down the stairs. He came to Esther and laid his massive head in her lap. Esther rubbed him fondly.

"Fine looking dog," Shane admired.

"He's great. We had him before the boys were born and we were afraid he would be jealous of the attention we gave to them, but he never was. He takes good care of them. He'll obey even little Martin." Esther started to say more, but tears flowed instead.

"What is it? Is something wrong?"

"Oh, no, no, nothing's wrong. It's just that I can hardly believe . . . believe all . . . all this. God is so good."

He nodded and reached for her hand. "Let's thank Him together."

The next eight days went by too fast. Shane's furlough had already been extended several times by his commanding officer. He praised the Lord for the days he had been given, but it was time to get back to work.

"Take care, Shane," Sam said, after his brother-in-law's bags were on the stage.

"I will, and you, too." Shaking Sam's hand, he glanced at Esther and said, "I'm glad you're the one that got my sister."

Sam swallowed hard and said, "I praise God that He gave her to me."

Shane turned to hug Esther goodbye. "Goodbye, Sis. I love you."

Esther stepped back and squeezed his hand. "I love you, Brother."

He said goodbye to all of the boys. "You fellows be good."

"We will," Mike assured him.

After shaking hands with Tom and Carol, Shane left.

That night, as Esther tucked Montana into bed, he said, "Momma, I want to be a soldier like Uncle Shane."

Esther smiled. "Maybe you can be, Monty."

"I love Uncle Shane," Martin said from the other side of the room.

"So do I," Esther said. "Let's thank the Lord for him."

"Can I do it, Momma?" Montana asked.

"Yes, son, you can."

"Dear Jesus, thank You for Uncle Shane. Thank You that he's a soldier. Amen."

Chapter 16

The Horse

As the month of July came to a close, work began to increase at the Silver Arrow and the Meadowlark. Soon it would be time to harvest the crops. Sam and Tom planned to use the money they got from the harvest to buy some cattle in the spring. Also, the horse auction was coming up and the corrals had to be finished.

The first Monday in August brought sad tidings to the Meadowlark. Tom's faithful horse Midnight was dying. Tom had raised Midnight from a colt. They had been together since Tom was eleven, but the stallion's days were running short. Tom took him out of the corral he shared with Dusty and put him in a box stall. It was easier to watch him and care for him there.

"How's he doing?" Carol asked.

Tom, standing in the stall, shook his head. Midnight was still on his feet, but his strength was failing. Tom gently rubbed his neck and toyed with the long mane that he had loved to watch flow in the wind when the horse ran.

"I knew the time would come," Tom said softly, as the horse nuzzled his hand. "It doesn't make it any easier, though."

The next day, Midnight was gone. Though they were busy, the two men took time to bury him.

Dusty missed his friend. The two horses had been together since they were young. He began to act strangely, sometimes pacing the corral all day. In his stall, he would whinny nervously, and he stopped eating.

"What's wrong with him?" Esther asked. She stood at the gate and watched Sam calm the horse.

"He misses Midnight." The bright gleam of spirit was gone from his horse's once fiery eyes, and the head usually held high dropped despairingly. Sam sighed. "I know, Dusty," he said soothingly.

Five days later they buried Dusty next to Midnight.

"They were good horses," Tom said as he used his shovel to smooth the dirt covering the two animals.

"Yep, the very best. The two best horses in the world," Sam said, quoting the phrase he and Tom had often used. "God was good to us to give us such great horses."

"I'm gonna miss Dusty," Mac said. All five of the boys had ridden Dusty often. He had become their horse.

"Me, too." Matt wiped away a tear.

Sam and Esther put their arms around the boys and they all cried.

Even Duke missed Dusty. He would look into the empty stall, his tail wagging hopefully. Then his tail would droop and he would go stand by Sam.

Sam thought often about the wonderful times the three of them had had. "Thank You, Lord, for so many wonderful and precious memories," Sam prayed.

The boys' birthday passed and Sam could hardly believe that they were now eight, seven, six, and five and that they had been in Montana a year already.

Soon the week of the auction came. Sam and Tom were eager, but the loss of Dusty and Midnight took some of the joy out of the event.

On the twenty-third of the month, cowboys and horses began arriving, crowding the streets of Miles City. Makeshift corrals that had been set up around town were full. The auction would take place on Thursday and Friday. Buyers spent the first part of the week looking over the horses and trying to decide which ones they were interested in.

"Are we ready to go to town, boys?" Sam asked on Monday morning.

"Yes sir," they all shouted. With the speed only boys know, they darted to the wagon.

Matthew grabbed the side of the wagon and swung over into the bed. Mike and Mac scrambled over the back, and the other two had to be lifted in. Once everyone was settled, the Goodtons and Sampsons headed down the dirt path.

The boys were thrilled at all the sights in town. Seasoned cowboys on their rugged ponies seemed to be everywhere. One group was having a contest, shooting at matches stuck to a hitching post several yards away. The corrals were filled with horses of every size and color. The boys picked out several and pointed them out to their parents. Sam and Esther praised each one.

After finding a place to put their wagons, they began to look around.

"Look there, Tom," Sam said. "A whole corral of Mustangs. Most men around town say that they're some of the best cowponies."

"Let's go take a look," Tom said.

"Where are they, Daddy?" Montana asked, too short to see over the crowd. "I can't see."

"I can't see, too," five-year-old Martin said.

"Well, we can fix that. Can't we, Sam?" Tom picked up Martin and put him on his shoulders. "Look, Marty, you're the tallest one!"

"Wait a minute," Sam said with a grin. He picked up Montana and set him on his shoulders. Then he stood back to back with Tom. "Which one's taller, Esther?"

"Montana is, but only because you're taller than Tom," she said with a smile.

"Switch, Daddy, switch," Marty begged. They did and he cried, "I'm tall now!"

Matthew looked up at his mother and teased, "Can I ride on your shoulder's, Mom?" Everyone laughed.

"Sorry, Matthew, but if you keep growing, you may be able to carry *me* soon," Esther said.

The twins, each holding on to one of Carol's hands, said simultaneously, "Look, there's an Appy horse!"

Sheriff Elwood rode an Appaloosa, but the word Appaloosa was too long for the younger boys, so all five called it an Appy. Every time they saw one, they pointed it out.

"I see it," Sam said. It was in the corral with the Mustangs. "Come on, let's go look."

By Wednesday, Sam and Tom had fifteen horses picked out. One was a hardy bay stallion, they would use to breed. Five were mares and the rest were geldings. One was the Appaloosa Mike and Mac had seen.

"This should be a good start," Sam said after lunch on Wednesday. Church would be starting in a couple of hours, so while the family was resting at the Kenneth's house, Tom and Sam were walking around the corrals one last time. "With our two saddle horses, the girls' mares, the eight wagon horses, and these fifteen, we'll have twenty-seven good horses."

"Praise the Lord!" Tom said.

"Yes. Tom, I've been thinking about something. There's a small band of range horses that roam our property. I've seen the stallion, and he's fine looking. Maybe we should consider catching him and branding him. That way—Tom, Tom, did you hear me?"

Tom was looking over Sam's shoulder, fascinated by something he saw there. Sam looked around but saw nothing very interesting. "Tommy, what're you looking at?"

"That horse."

"Where? What horse?"

"That one, right over there. Isn't he beautiful?"

Sam was beginning to wonder if Tom was suffering from heat stroke, but then he saw it, too. "You mean that tall chestnut over there."

"Yeah, come on. Let's take a look at him."

The chestnut was the only horse in the corral. Several men were standing at the fence, gazing at the magnificent animal.

"He *is* pretty," Sam agreed, studying the animal. "All of sixteen hands high, if not taller. Wonder what breed he is."

"I can answer that question, gentleman," a young cowboy said. "He's an American Saddle Horse. You don't see many of them out here. My boss is trying to get them spread out as show horses."

"Any good for ranch work?" Sam asked.

"Some are, but I wouldn't recommend it for this fellow," he said, pointing toward the prancing horse. "He's for showing and breeding."

"He's a fine looking horse," Sam said.

"Thank you." The man said goodbye and began to wander around the corral to answer questions.

"I want that horse, Sam," Tom said.

"Yeah, me too, but he's no good for us right now. Besides, he probably costs almost as much as all our horses put together."

"He reminds me of Midnight," Tom said, as if he had not heard Sam speak.

"Tom, you're not seriously thinking about getting him are you?" Sam asked nervously.

"I am."

"Tom, it's not practical. We have no use for him. He needs to be in a place where he can be shown. If we get him, we wouldn't dare use him for ranch work, and he'd just spend his life in a corral."

"I know, but surely we could use him for something. We were talking about breeding Tennessee Walkers. Why not this kind instead?"

"Not now. We're not ready for that yet."

Tom sighed. "I'll think about it."

They were a few feet from the corral when Fred Trenton stepped up to them. They had come to Miles City on the same wagon train. He was a selfish, arrogant man that no one really liked to be around. He had a great deal of money, but it did not make him happy, and he did not like other people to be happy. Nothing was ever his fault. He always found someone else to blame for his troubles.

"Hello, sirs," he said.

"Hello, Mr. Trenton," Tom responded politely.

"Afternoon, Mr. Trenton," Sam said.

"Did I hear you gentlemen say you are considering buying this horse?"

"Yes," Tom answered quickly.

"Well, I must tell you that I plan on buying this horse and showing him. I am prepared to pay a high price for him. So if you wish to battle for this horse when the auction takes place, I encourage you to come well-prepared." He turned and walked away.

Chapter 17

Auction Time

"That horse won't make him happy," Sam said.

"You're right," Tom agreed.

"Then why do you think that this horse will make *you* happy, Tommy?"

Tom had no answer.

That night, Sam told Esther of his concern. "I've never seen his judgment so clouded. It's not that the horse is bad. It's that he's not practical for us right now. He's gonna cost Tom a bundle of money that he could use for his cattle next year."

"What do you think we can do?"

"Pray."

Thursday morning the whole town was out to see the auction. Everyone had heard that Trenton and Sampson were bidding on the American Saddle Horse. Most were there to see which one would win.

The first animal up for sale was the chestnut horse. Sam and Esther had been praying that Tom would do what the Lord wanted. If that meant getting the horse, they would support him. If not, they prayed he would leave it alone.

"Folks, what am I bid for this fine American Saddle Horse? He's the first one of his kind to be auctioned off in Miles City. Now what am I bid?" The minute the auctioneer named a number, Trenton bid.

Sam glanced toward Tom, along with everyone else. Tom looked at the horse and pursed his lips. He said nothing even though a murmur rippled through the crowd. Within two minutes, Trenton owned the horse.

Sam stepped up to Tom and put his arm around him.

"Why?"

Tom gave a lopsided smile. "I knew God didn't want me to have that horse, but I didn't want to listen to Him. I couldn't sleep last night. I told myself that it was just excitement, but I knew it wasn't. In my morning devotions I was reading in Luke, where the rich man wanted to tear down his barns and build bigger ones. He wanted to store up his harvest and take it easy. But God called him a fool, and said, 'this night thy soul shall be required of thee:' Then the Bible said, 'So is he that layeth up treasure for himself, and is not rich toward God.'

"That man was not robbed *of* his possessions," Tom explained. "He was robbed *by* his possessions. God blessed his crops, and instead of using them for God, he kept them for himself. God has blessed me, and I was about to use it for me and not for what He wanted. The money He's sent me is to buy cattle. If I had disobeyed, my peace, joy, and right standing with God would have been stolen. Things are good to have, but that horse would have had *me*. Thanks for praying that I'd make the right decision. Though disobedience won't make me lose my salvation, it will stop the blessings of God, and mess up my testimony."

Sam slapped his friend on the back. "Thank the Lord, buddy. I'm glad you listened to God."

The next Monday the Sheriff rode up to Tom's house.

"Hello, Sheriff."

"Howdy, Tom. I have some bad news. I'm afraid you're going to have to come to town with me. You know that horse that Mr. Trenton bought? Well, it went lame today. He's pressing charges against you. Says you did something to the horse."

Tom gave an exasperated sigh and merely shook his head. Carol clasped her hands worriedly.

"I feel terrible about this, Mr. Sampson. I don't think that you did anything, but you better come with me. Right now, the blacksmith is looking the horse over to see what happened."

"Of course, Sheriff, I'll come."

They stopped at the Silver Arrow and Sam went to town with them.

They went straight to the blacksmith's place. Sam and Tom did not know the blacksmith's full name. The man called himself only Murphy. He was an expert with metal, and he knew how to doctor animals.

When Sam, Tom, and Sheriff Elwood walked in, Murphy was kneeling by the injured horse. His hands were gentle as he examined the right foreleg.

Fred Trenton glared at Tom. "So," he began hotly, "since you couldn't have him, you made it so no one could have him. You'll pay for this. Mark my words. I don't know what you did but—"

"He didn't do anything," Murphy interrupted.

Trenton's face, already red with anger, turned a deeper red. "What do you mean?"

"Mr. Trenton, when you sent for me to look at this horse, I looked at your corral. It was uneven and full of rocks. Probably there are a few holes in it. Not a good place for any horse, let alone a fine animal like this. Were you lunging the horse when he started limping?"

"Well, I . . . I was . . . well . . . yeah, but what does that have to do with anything?"

"Simple, *you* did this to your horse. When I got to your place, he was covered with sweat. You must've had him running long and hard. This horse was tired and he probably lost his footing. His leg is sprained, but with time and care he'll be alright."

"You mean he'll be just like new?" Trenton asked.

Murphy shook his head. "No, you won't be able to show him and I wouldn't breed him."

"Then what good is he?"

Murphy stood up. "Oh, he'd make a great riding horse for a child or a girl. He's a gentle creature and a beauty."

Trenton sputtered. "You mean I paid all that money for him and now he's no good? It can't be! What do I do? It's not right!"

"Well, I'll tell you," Murphy said. "I'll give you a hundred dollars for him. I know it's not what you paid but—"

"I'll take it. Send me the money." He glared at Tom. "I still say you did something. Mark my words, I'll never do business or have anything to do with a Sampson again." He turned on his heel and left.

Elwood sighed. "I guess that's the end. Sorry I had to bring you out here, Tom."

"That's alright, Sheriff. If it's okay, we'll go home." Elwood nodded.

Before he left, Tom stepped up to the horse and began to pet him.

"He'll make a great riding horse for my daughter," the blacksmith said.

Tom shook his hand. "Thanks, Murphy."

Sam and Tom mounted and started back down the road. Tom was quiet.

"You okay, Tommy?"

"Yeah, but I wish Mr. Trenton wasn't mad at me."

"I know. Keep him in your prayers and see if the Lord will change his heart."

"I will. So long buddy, and thanks for coming with me," Tom said as he turned down the trail to the Meadowlark.

"You're welcome, friend," Sam said and turned toward home.

Carol ran out to meet Tom and he smiled at her and dismounted. Putting his arms around her, he said, "Everything's taken care of." She sighed happily.

As he put his horse away, Tom told his wife all that happened. "Mr. Trenton is angry, but he's not going to press charges," he finished.

"Praise the Lord," Carol said.

"Yes, God worked it all out. I almost disobeyed Him, and He protected me anyway. It seems like He would say, 'You're the one that got into this mess. See if you can get out.' I'm so glad that He's not like that. On the way home, I thought about the time Moses wanted to see God's glory. God hid him in the clift of the rock and passed by him and called Himself 'The LORD, The LORD God, merciful and gracious, longsuffering, and abundant in goodness and truth,' When God wanted Moses to know something about Himself, one of the first things He said was that He was a merciful God."

Carol smiled. "Today, He showed us His mercy."

Late that night, a stranger rode up to the Meadowlark. His sweat-covered Mustang stopped in front of the porch. A tired two-year-old colt followed them. The man leaned over the horn of his saddle, weak and obviously hurt. He tried to call out, but lost his grip on the saddle horn and fell to the ground.

Tom and Carol were in the big room when they heard a horse whinny. Tom was instantly alert.

Carol looked up from her mending. "What is it?"

Tom strapped his holster around his waist. "None of our horses have a whinny like that," he whispered. "Wonder what a stranger would be doing here this time of night. Stay away from the doors and windows." Tom checked his pistol before opening the door to the dining room and creeping up to the front window.

"Careful, Tom," Carol whispered.

He peeked out. When he saw the figure lying in the yard, he holstered his pistol and hurried out to the man. Turning him over gently, he saw a bullet wound in his right arm. He checked the man's pulse.

"Carol!"

Carol came running out. "Oh, my, I'll get the extra room ready," she said hastily. "Can you carry him in alone?"

"I think so." The limp body was dead weight. Praying for strength, Tom lifted the man carefully.

Soon, the injured man was on the bed and Carol was wrapping a bandage around the wounded arm. "He's lost a lot of blood, but I think he'll be alright. You best call for Sam and have him get the doctor."

Tom took his rifle and stepped outside. He fired once, waited ten seconds, and fired two quick shots. Tom knew Sam would be over shortly.

In less than six hours, Doctor James had come and gone, giving them a good report. Though the injured man was still unconscious, he would most likely recover.

Sheriff Elwood was there. He had been looking through the man's personal papers when he whistled.

"What'd you find, Sheriff?" Tom asked.

"He is an Indian agent from Billings, Montana. His name is Brady Owens. Wonder what happened to him. Mind if I stay what's left of the night?"

"Not at all."

The next afternoon, Owens awoke. "Where am I?" he asked, dazed.

"You're at the Meadowlark Ranch near Miles City, Montana. I'm Sheriff Keith Elwood. Can you tell me what happened?"

"Yeah." He sat up in the bed. "Brady Owens is the name, Indian Agent. I was on my way to Miles City to meet with Jim Clifford when someone bushwhacked me. Must've happened about, oh, ten miles back up the trail. Important things are happening in Billings, possibly some major peace treaties to be signed. Guess someone's not too happy about it. I remember very little about what happened after I got shot. My horse must've brought me here. Much obliged to the folks for taking me in."

Elwood opened the bedroom door and motioned to Tom and Carol. "These are the folks." Owens repeated his thanks.

On Wednesday, he was well enough to go to town. Tom saddled the Mustang and brought it from the barn. The colt, black except for a long white blaze down the middle of his face, was frisky and feeling his oats. He ran around the yard for a few minutes before coming to stand behind the other horse.

"Sure would like to pay you folks for what you've done for me."

"No need for that," Tom handed him the reins.

Owens smiled and looked at the colt. "Do you have a good saddle horse?"

"Yes," Tom answered, thinking of the quarter-horse he had brought from Indiana.

"How old is he?"

"Oh, about ten or eleven."

"Well, if you won't take money, will you take the colt?"

Tom and Carol looked at one another in surprise.

"An Indian chief gave me three two-year-old colts, one for me and two to sell. I sold one and was gonna sell this one in Miles City. Will you take him in payment for all you've done? I insist."

Tom looked at the colt. He thought of Midnight and nodded. "Thank you."

"You're welcome." With his good arm Owens mounted, and he and Elwood headed for town.

Tom slipped a rope around the colt's neck and led him back to the corral.

"God is good. His mercy doesn't give me what I deserve, and His grace gives me what I don't deserve."

Chapter 18

Neighbors

September brought beautiful weather. When the Goodtons and Sampsons stopped their team in front of the church on Sunday morning, Jonathon Davidson and his wife Jenny walked up to them. Jonathon managed the land office. He had sold land to Sam and Tom when they first arrived in Miles City.

"Hey, Sam, I've got news for you."

"What's that, Jonathon?" Sam asked as he jumped down.

"You've got neighbors, Randall and Barb Holte."

Esther's face lit up. "Really, where?"

"They moved in right next to your side of the ranch," Jenny explained. "I remember when we got our first neighbors and how glad we were."

"While they were on their way out here, some friends in Miles City built them a house," Jonathan said. "They moved in three days ago. Their house isn't but two miles from yours. I waited until it was all final to tell you." He shook his head. "I've had too many deals like that fall through, so I don't bank on it until it's all said and done."

Sam grinned. "I understand."

Just before the service started, an unfamiliar couple came in. Since the church was almost full, they had to sit in the last row. Sam wondered if they were the Holtes.

At the end of the service Sam tried to get back to meet them, but by the time he got to the back door, they were gone.

"Why'd you leave in such a hurry, Sammy?" Tom asked.

Sam explained to him about their neighbors.

"Hey, that's great! Maybe sometime this week we can get over there to see them."

"I don't know. We're harvesting this week, 'member?"

Tom winced. "Oh yeah."

"You never know, though," Sam continued. "Sure would like to. Maybe we can talk to them tonight." However, they did not get a chance that night to speak to them.

Tuesday, while Sam and Tom were riding out to the field, they heard a strange sound.

"What was that?" Tom asked, his right hand dropping to grab his rifle from its scabbard. Duke let out a low growl.

Sam was quiet as he tried to discern where the noise had come from. Again they heard it.

"A cow?" Tom asked.

"Sounds like it. Come on. It came from up that way." Sam checked his pistol and cautiously made his way to where the cry had sounded. Tom followed close behind. They rounded a corner and saw a lone cow caught in a mud hole. Four feet away was a break in the fence.

"Well, I guess this is practice time for us." Sam opened his lariat. He swung it around a few times to get loosened up and then aimed the loop for the cow. He missed.

Tom laughed. "I guess practice would be a good thing for you."

Sam grinned wryly and recoiled his rope. "Okay, Mr. Sure Throw, let's see you try."

"I was afraid you would suggest that." Tom opened up his rope, aimed for the cow, and the lariat settled neatly around her neck.

"What do you know?" Tom said, amazed at his success.

Sam's grin widened and he tried once again. The second time he too hit the mark.

After securing the ends of their lariats to their saddle horns, they began to haul the cow out. Soon it was once again on solid ground.

"Wonder who she belongs to," Tom pondered.

"Don't know. Keep a tight hold on her so she don't get away." Sam dismounted and told Duke to sit and stay so that he would not frighten the cow.

Sam approached the mud-covered animal. She was tired from struggling to get out of the mud hole and made no move to get away from him. After rubbing her head, he began to wipe the mud from her left flank. He found what he was looking for.

"The brand is Bar H," he informed Tom.

"Bar H . . . Hey, would that be the Holtes?"

"I'd say so. They own the land on the other side of this fence." Sam wiped his hands. "Let me fix this break and we'll take her back. The next gate is only a few hundred yards up the line."

After mending the fence and stopping at a spring to water the exhausted cow, they rode for the Holte's house.

When they entered the yard, a tall man with blonde hair came out of the barn.

"Howdy," he called out.

"Howdy," Tom answered. "We found this cow stuck in a mud hole. Does she belong to you?"

"Yes, she does. I just found out she was missing and was getting ready to saddle my horse and go find her. Much obliged."

"You're quite welcome," Sam assured him as he and Tom dismounted. "The name is Sam Goodton. I own the Silver Arrow."

"Oh, the ranch right next to ours." He shook Sam's hand. "I'm Randall Holte. Pleased to meet you."

"This is Tom Sampson. He owns the Meadowlark."

"Nice to meet you," Tom said. "Where you from?"

"Georgia. My wife Barb and I had some friends that moved out here two years ago. They wrote and told us about this wonderful place called Montana. The more they wrote, the more Barb and I wanted to come. We prayed about it and were assured it was the right thing. Our friends offered to build our house for us, so all we had to do was come. And here we are."

"You folks are saved then?" Tom asked.

"Sure are. What about you two?"

"Yes, we are," Sam said.

"I thought I saw you folks in church. We had so much work to do we didn't have time to stay and fellowship last Sunday, and both services we had trouble with the wagon on the way to church."

An instant friendship was struck between the Holtes, Goodtons, and Sampsons. The next Sunday they had lunch together. Sam and Tom were elated to find out that Mr. Holte was a cattle expert. They plied him with questions. They were eating dinner together one Saturday night when Sam asked Mr. Holte what kind of cattle he preferred.

"Well, I like Herefords. That's what I raised in Georgia, but out here they have some problems. It's not a real hearty breed. The West can be a bit too rugged for them. I've done some research, and several ranchers have been breeding Texas Longhorns with Herefords. You get the good meat from the

Hereford and the ruggedness of the Longhorn. Lord willing that's what I'll be doing. Once the railroad gets out here, I'll be shipping my prize Hereford bull up here." Mr. Holte grinned. "I miss that monster."

His wife Barb nodded. "His name is Uno. That's Spanish for 'one.' When my Honey first saw him, he said, 'That has got to be the greatest bull I've ever seen. He's the one we need'. So, since that bull was 'the one,' we named him Uno."

"I sure would like to see him," Tom said. "Soon as the railroad gets in, Sam and I are going to go look for a good bull. We'll start in Rapid City and check the area around there."

"If you stay on the west side of the Missouri River in South Dakota, you'll find a lot of cattle ranches. To the east of the river is mostly farmland."

"That's what we've heard," Sam said.

Barb Holte turned to face Sam's boys. "Are you boys going to work with cattle when you grow up?"

"Yes, ma'am!" Their faces beamed with anticipation.

Esther smiled at her sons. The thought of starting their own herd thrilled her almost as much as it did Sam. She was content here in Montana.

Chapter 19

A Mother's Love

"It's mine!"

"No, it's mine! I found it first!"

"No! Give it to me!"

Esther dropped her knitting and raced outside as the sounds of war increased.

Montana and Martin were both clinging to a rock and each was pulling with all his might.

"Boys, boys," Esther scolded. When she pulled them apart, the precious stone fell to the ground. Both boys tried to dive for it, but Esther held them back.

"What's going on?"

The boys were silent.

"I asked you both a question. What is going on? Why are you fighting?"

"Um," Montana began slowly, but said nothing more.

"Yes?" Esther asked.

"I found the rock first!" Martin exploded. That set off a chain reaction.

"No you didn't! I found it!" Monty yelled.

Esther shook her head in dismay and pulled the boys over to the porch. *Please, help me, Lord*, she prayed.

"Sit down," she told the boys firmly.

"Aw, but, Mom," they moaned in unison.

"Sit down."

They reluctantly obeyed.

"Now, I want you both to listen to me and not interrupt. There were two sisters in the Bible. They both had something that the other wanted. Leah wanted to be loved by a certain person. That person loved Rachel, Leah's sister, but Rachel wasn't happy. She wanted children. Leah had children, but she wasn't happy either. Their home was a mess and though they both ended up getting what they wanted, they died in the process. Rachel did have children, but she died during childbirth. Leah finally got to be near the person she longed for, but it was only in death that they were side by side." She sighed. "Things don't make people happy," she told them gently. "Only the Lord can make a person happy." She picked up the rock and looked at it. "It *is* beautiful, but is it worth you boys being angry and mad at each other? Is it worth your friendship?"

Montana and Martin were quiet. They both wanted the rock, but they knew their mom was right.

"You boys need to apologize."

They looked down.

"Don't look away from me," she scolded. "Montana, Martin, I said that you need to apologize."

Montana spoke first. "I'm sorry, Marty."

Martin shrugged. "I'm sorry, Monty."

"What do you think you should do?" Esther asked.

Montana rolled his eyes. Reluctantly he gave his younger brother a half-hug. Martin returned it with the same lack of exuberance, but when the hug was over the tension was gone.

"Good," Esther said.

"Mom," Montana said, "I'm sorry I got angry. Martin can have the rock."

"I don't want it anymore," Martin said. "Mom, would you like to have it?"

Esther smiled. "I'll tell you what. We'll put it on the mantle above the fireplace. That way we'll be reminded of the lesson we learned today. Things don't make you happy. Romans 14:17 says, 'For the kingdom of God is not meat and drink; but righteousness, and peace, and joy in the Holy Ghost.'"

"Okay!" the boys chorused and then raced off together.

Esther had just settled down to her knitting when she heard a ruckus coming from the back yard.

What now? she thought. She lay her knitting aside once again and quickly made her way to the yard where the three older boys were working. She opened the back door and listened.

"I say, I should rake and you two make them into nice piles," Matthew stated.

"No, it will work better if we all rake," Mike argued.

"You're both wrong," Mac put in, "I think two should rake and one pile."

"Now, I'm the oldest," Matthew reminded, "and I say—"

"You may be the oldest," Mike interrupted, "but I dare say I know more about this than either—"

"Well," Mac said, laying his rake down, "I'm the strongest so—"

"I say you *all* are wrong." Esther stepped into view.

The three boys froze. Surprise turned to shame as they realized they had been overheard.

"Mike, go to your room and wait for me. MacShane, go to my room and wait."

The twins nodded and headed for the house.

"I'm sorry, Mom," Matthew said. "I should have known better."

Esther took his hand and they went for a walk.

"Matthew, that was wrong. You think that because you're older you are wiser and you know everything. You tend to boss your brothers around. You like to be the leader, but you're going about it wrong. Who do you think was the greatest leader in the Bible?"

"Jesus."

"I agree, but what made Jesus such a good leader?"

Matthew thought for a few minutes. "Because He was God?"

"That's one reason," Esther said, "but not the only one. He submitted to authority, His Father. Jesus said in John 6:38, 'For I came down from heaven, not to do mine own will, but the will of him that sent me.' In John 8:29, He

said, 'I do always those things that please him.'
God said that He was pleased with His Son.

"There is another reason that Jesus was
such a good leader. He was also a servant to
the people. Do you remember when Jesus
washed the disciples' feet?"

Matthew nodded.

"Jesus said in Mark 10:45 that He 'came
not to be ministered unto, but to minister, and
to give his life a ransom for many.' And the
second chapter of Philippians reminds us of
how much Jesus lowered Himself to come and
be our Saviour. It says that He 'made himself
of no reputation, and took upon him the form of
a servant, and was made in the likeness of
men: And being found in fashion as a man, he
humbled himself, and became obedient unto
death, even the death of the cross.'"

"Wow," Matthew said. "Jesus sure did
lower Himself. He was a servant, and that's
what made Him such a great leader."

"Yes, and the next three verses tell of how
God rewarded Jesus. 'Wherefore God also
hath highly exalted him, and given him a name
which is above every name: That at the name
of Jesus every knee should bow, of things in
heaven, and things in earth, and things under

the earth; And that every tongue should confess that Jesus Christ is Lord, to the glory of God the Father.'"

They stopped walking and Esther looked into the eyes of her oldest son. "I know that you want to be a good leader, but it will never happen if you don't submit to authority and if you don't serve."

"I'll try, Mom," Matthew promised.

"There's a rock sitting on the mantle above the fireplace," Esther said. "When you see it, think about the fact that Jesus, our Rock, was a servant. In John 13:14-15 Christ said, 'If I then, your Lord and Master, have washed your feet; ye also ought to wash one another's feet. For I have given you an example, that ye should do as I have done to you.'"

A few minutes later, Esther walked into the twins' room.

Mike jumped up and ran to her. "I'm so sorry, Mom," he said. "I'm sorry."

She led him to the bed and they sat down.

"Mike, I heard you say that you know more than your brothers."

He hung his head. "That's not true," he admitted.

"Who was the wisest man in the Bible?"

"King Solomon."

"Yes, but do you know that even King Solomon did a very foolish thing. As Solomon got older, he began to fellowship with those who did not believe in the true God. Soon he began worshipping false gods. The Bible tells us in 1 Kings 11:4 that 'it came to pass, when Solomon was old, that his wives turned away his heart after other gods: and his heart was not perfect with the LORD his God, as was the heart of David his father.'"

Mike's face was the picture of disbelief. "Why? He knew Who the real God was."

"Yes, but it takes more than knowing Who God is. You must know Him personally."

"I'm saved. I know Who God is, and I know Him personally."

"True. The world has wisdom and not godliness because they don't know God, but this also applies to Christians. You must develop that relationship. The Bible says in Proverbs 9:10 that 'The fear of the LORD is the beginning of wisdom: and the knowledge of the holy is understanding.'

"Where do you learn about God?" Esther asked.

"From the Bible and going to church and prayer."

"Yes. Sitting on the mantle above the fireplace is a rock. A rock is solid. Psalms 119:89 says that God's Word 'is settled in heaven.' God's Word is solid. When you look at that rock, remember that solid wisdom comes from God."

Esther patted his arm and went to see MacShane. He, like the others, quickly apologized.

Esther, as she had already done throughout the day of arguments, prayed silently for wisdom to help her son.

"I shouldn't have said what I said," MacShane admitted.

"You're right, Mac," she said.

"I feel really bad. I hope I never get mad again, and I hope I *never* brag about me again."

"Shane, who was one of the strongest men in the Bible?"

"Samson!"

Esther smiled at his enthusiasm. "Yes. He was a strong hero, but as you know, he ended up pretty bad."

"Yeah, I always wondered why that happened."

"It was because he let his passions get in the way."

"What's passions?" he asked.

"Umm, let's see. How would you describe passions? Well, let me put it like this. He let his desires get in the way. In your case, your desire is to let everyone know how strong you are, but you must remember that being big and tough isn't important. Being what God wants is important. Who made you strong?"

"God did."

"Right. So when you say you're strong and pick on others, is that right?"

He shook his head. "No."

"Being strong spiritually is more important than being strong physically. Paul tells us in Ephesians to 'be strong in the Lord, and in the power of his might.' In Genesis, Jacob said that his son Joseph's strength came from the Lord. He said that 'the arms of his hands were made strong by the hands of the mighty God of Jacob;' And in Proverbs 3:5 we are told to 'Trust in the LORD with all thine heart; and lean not unto thine own understanding.'"

MacShane smiled. "Those are good verses. I need to put my trust in God's strength and not mine!"

"Yes, that's right. There's a rock on the mantle above the fireplace. When you see it, remember that God is our Rock and our Strength. In Psalms 18, David said, 'The LORD is my rock, and my fortress, and my deliverer; my God, my strength, in whom I will trust; my buckler, and the horn of my salvation, and my high tower.'"

Esther sent the three boys back out to the yard and watched as they asked forgiveness of each other. Within a few minutes, they were laughing and working together. She then went to the front door and watched her two younger sons playing.

It was only after the boys went to bed that night that Sam noticed the sparkling rock on the mantle.

"What's this?"

Esther chuckled. She told him about the "conflicts" of the day and how that rock somehow managed to fit into every situation. "So," she ended, "it's a reminder."

Sam looked at his wife and then back at the rock. Tears formed in his eyes. Esther was such a godly woman, a wife that he did not deserve. *Thank You, Heavenly Father, for my Esther*, he prayed. Aloud he said, "I love you, Esther honey, and I'm thankful for you."

Chapter 20

At the Cross

As October started, the weather was the best it had been in a long time. Sam and his family, enjoying the pleasant days, decided to go to town.

"Howdy," Steve welcomed them as they entered his store. "I see you brought the whole crew this time."

"Yeah," Sam smiled down at his boys. He looked back to the storekeeper. "Any news on how the railroad is doing?"

"Yes, good news. They're saying it'll be here by November."

The railroad not only reached Miles City by November but it laid track even beyond the city. On the 15th of November, the first engine carrying passengers was set to arrive.

Since the fourteenth was a Sunday, all those not living in town made arrangements to stay the night after church so that they could greet the train the next day. Monday afternoon a crowd gathered around the train station, a building that had been finished only a couple of days before.

Welcome banners hung everywhere and a band was there, ready to play a rousing song of welcome.

"This is so exciting!" Matt exclaimed. Sam smiled and put his arm around him. He motioned for the other boys to come closer.

"Listen, boys." He knelt and gathered them around him. "I want you to watch this very carefully. You may not fully understand it now, but you're watching history in the making. God has given us the special privilege to see this. Like Matthew said, it is exciting. Let's not forget that God in His mercy has let us be here to see it all happen. Okay?"

"Yes, sir."

Sam's smile widened as he watched his sons looking on with eager eyes.

Thank You, Lord, Sam prayed. *You've already been so good to us. This is another wonderful blessing. Please help us to never take Your blessings for granted.* He turned in a complete circle, taking in all the sights before looking up at the schedule marked on the outside wall of the station.

The train was to pull in at 2:30 P. M. Sam checked his watch and saw there was only thirty minutes to go. He reached down to pat Duke who, sensing the excitement, was trembling with anticipation. His nose wiggled as he sniffed the air for any sign of trouble.

"Good boy," Sam whispered.

At 2:25 a loud whistle startled the onlookers. Shading their eyes from the sun, they looked toward the east.

"I see it!" MacShane shouted.

Across the open plain, the black steam engine rolled toward them. The crowd began applauding. The steady chugging noise grew louder as the train drew nearer and nearer. With a loud hiss and a squeal of the brakes, it came to a stop. The station clock read 2:28.

The conductor leaned out the window and shouted, "Not only did this here engine come all the way from Illinois, she got here two minutes early!"

Everyone cheered and Duke barked. They became silent as the president of the railroad company emerged from one of the cars. He looked out over the crowd.

"Ladies and Gentlemen, this is a great day for Miles City. The coming of the iron horse will bring great industries. It will provide you with a safe and quick means of transportation to various places around our grand country. We will ship your produce and your cattle efficiently." He paused and motioned to a banner that said, "WELCOME RAILROAD, WE'RE GLAD YOU'RE HERE."

"Our wish," he continued, "is that you good people will always be glad and proud that we are *your* railroad company. Thank you all."

There was another rousing cheer and the band started to play again.

"That was thrilling!" Esther exclaimed on the way home. "Did you boys have fun?" she asked, turning around to face them.

"It was great!" Montana said.

"I liked it when they blew the whistle," Mac told them.

"I liked the smoke!" said Martin.

Matthew nodded, "I liked the whole thing, but especially the fact that soon you and Uncle Tom can go get some cattle."

His dad was silent for a moment. "Yes, that's something Tom and I have to figure out. Hey, Tom!"

"Yeah," Tom answered. Driving in front of the Goodton's wagon, he turned to look at Sam.

"When you wanting to leave for South Dakota?"

"I'm thinking about next March."

As December came in, the weather no longer held the Indian Summer feel. Six-year-old Montana sighed as if the world was coming to an end. He had been ill, and Sam and Esther had decided that he needed to stay inside out of the cold. He was standing on a chair and looking out the front window. Wrapped in a heavy blanket, he watched his brothers and the dog play in the snow. Suddenly, he had a thought and jumped down from the chair.

Esther was in the kitchen when she heard the plinking of piano keys.

"Who is that?" she wondered. She stepped out of the kitchen, looked toward the piano, and smiled. Montana had folded the blanket, placed it on the bench, and crawled on top of it. From there, he could see and reach the keys. When he found the note he was looking for, he began searching for another. He was concentrating so hard that he did not see her watching him.

He figured out the notes he wanted and tried to play them in a smooth phrase. Tears came to his mother's eyes as she realized that he was trying to play "At the Cross" the way she played it. He made several mistakes, but within twenty minutes he had learned the verse and chorus. Satisfied, he jumped off the bench, picked up the blanket, wrapped it around him, and walked toward the kitchen. It was only then that he saw his mom, but he was still unaware that she had been watching him.

"Mom, I'm hungry. Can I have a biscuit?"

"Sure, Soldier. Come sit down at the table."

After she had poured him some milk, she opened the breadbox, took out a leftover biscuit, and spread it with butter and homemade strawberry jelly. After fixing a second one for herself, she took them to the table. They had prayer and then enjoyed their snack.

"I heard you playing the piano, Monty. It sounded very good."

He blushed, embarrassed that someone had heard him playing. "Thank you." He looked down at his biscuit for a minute. "Mom, what does that song mean?"

Esther looked up at her son, surprised at the question. "What do you mean?"

"Why do you and Daddy sometimes cry when you sing it, and why do you like to sing it? What does it mean?"

"Well, wait just a minute and let me get my Bible."

As Esther hurried into the living room to get the family Bible, she prayed that God would give her wisdom. She returned to the table and sat by her son.

"The first verse of the song goes like this:
'Alas and did my Saviour bleed?
And did my Sovereign die?
Would He devote that sacred head
For such a worm as I?'

"Jesus Christ is God's Son," Esther explained. "He was, is, and always will be God. First John 4:14 says, 'the Father sent the Son to be the Saviour of the world.' We needed a Saviour because we are all sinners. Romans 3:23 says that 'all have sinned, and come short of the glory of God;' And we learn from the first part of Romans 6:23 that the only payment for sin is death. So, Jesus Christ willingly came to earth and died for you and me. That's what the first verse of the song is talking about. Jesus, our Saviour, bled and died to pay sin's penalty."

"What about that 'worm' part?"

"Man is referred to as a worm in the book of Isaiah. It means we are lowly and unworthy. Isaiah 41:14 says, 'Fear not, thou worm Jacob, and ye men of Israel; I will help thee, saith the LORD, and thy redeemer, the Holy One of Israel.' The songwriter was saying that it is amazing that a holy God would die for sinful men, women, boys, and girls. Do you understand?"

When Montana nodded, Esther continued. "The second verse says,

'Was it for crimes that I have done,
He groaned upon the tree?
Amazing pity! grace unknown!
And love beyond degree!'

"Here we are told again that Jesus died on the cross for our sins. Colossians 2:14 talks about Jesus 'Blotting out the handwriting of ordinances that was against us, which was contrary to us,' and says that He 'took it out of the way, nailing it to his cross;' Second Corinthians 5:21 says that God 'made him to

be sin for us, who knew no sin; that we might
be made the righteousness of God in him.'
And I Peter 2:24 says that Christ 'bare our sins
in his own body on the tree, that we, being
dead to sins, should live unto righteousness:
by whose stripes ye were healed.'"

"Why?" Montana suddenly asked. Tears
were in his eyes as he thought of Jesus dying
because of someone else's sins.

"Why what?"

"Why did He die? He was perfect. Jesus
never sinned. Why did He let them kill Him?"

"Because Jesus loves us. If He had not
died, we would have to die and also go to hell.
Jesus doesn't want us to go there. Second
Peter 3:9 says that the Lord is 'not willing that
any should perish, but that all should come to
repentance.' The writer of Hebrews tells us
that Jesus was willing to die because He
wanted us. Hebrews 12:2 says that He
endured the cross 'for the joy that was set
before him.' The joy that was set before Him is
those who trust Him as their Saviour. And
John 3:16 says that 'God so loved the world,
that he gave his only begotten Son, that
whosoever believeth in him should not perish,
but have everlasting life.'

"The third verse of the song goes,
   'Well might the sun in darkness hide,
     And shut His glories in.
  When Christ the mighty Maker died,
     For man the creature's sin.'

"It is reminding us that when Jesus died, darkness came over the earth. Luke 23:44 says that 'it was about the sixth hour, and there was a darkness over all the earth until the ninth hour.'

"The words of the fourth verse are,
   'Thus might I hide my blushing face,
     While His dear cross appears.
  Dissolve my heart in thankfulness,
     And melt mine eyes to tears.'

"We should be ashamed of our sin when we think of His cross, and be thankful for what He has done for us. Monty, there is nothing we can do to repay Him. God had every right to deny us a home in Heaven, but He didn't. He made a way for us. The only thing we have to do is accept what He did on Calvary to save us and wash away our sins. There's no good thing we could do to pay the Lord back for what He has done. According to Isaiah 64:6, 'But we are all as an unclean thing, and all our righteousnesses are as filthy rags; and we all do fade as a leaf; and our iniquities, like the wind, have taken us away.' We cannot get forgiveness and salvation on our own. Titus 3:5 explains, 'Not by works of righteousness which we have done, but according to his mercy he saved us, by the washing of regeneration, and renewing of the Holy Ghost;'

"The chorus to 'At the Cross' shows us the plan of salvation.

'At the cross, at the cross,
Where I first saw the light.
And the burden of my heart rolled way.
It was there by faith
I received my sight,
And now I am happy all the day.'

"To get salvation, simply realize you are a sinner and ask Jesus to save you. Romans 10:13 says, 'For whosoever shall call upon the name of the Lord shall be saved.' And in Acts 16:31, Paul and Silas said, 'Believe on the Lord Jesus Christ, and thou shalt be saved,'

"The last verse reminds us that there is nothing we can do to earn salvation. It also reminds those that are saved that we should live for God out of a thankful heart; not to get His forgiveness, but because we are forgiven.

'But drops of grief can ne'r repay,

The debt of love I owe:
Here, Lord, I give myself away,
'Tis all that I can do.'

Montana swallowed the last of his biscuit, and considered what his mother had told him.

"Momma, I'm a sinner. So that means Jesus died for me, right?"

"Yes, Monty."

He was silent for a few moments. Then he smiled. "Jesus loves me, and Jesus died for me. Boy, that's great. I want to get saved. Can I, even though I'm just a little boy?"

"Yes."

Montana bowed his head. "Dear Jesus, thank You for dying on the cross for me. Thank You for thinking of me way back before I was born. I believe on the Lord Jesus Christ. Please save me and forgive me of my sin. I'm glad You died for me. Please save me. Thank You. Amen." He looked up and said, "I understand that song now, Mommy. I understand, and I see why you and Dad love it."

Chapter 21

Cattle

M arch third saw Sam and Tom getting ready to leave in search of cattle. Before they mounted their horses, Tom said, "Let's pray before we leave."

"You go ahead, Tom," Sam answered.

"Dear Lord, we want to first thank You for all that You have done. Secondly, we ask for safety for our families . . ."

As he prayed, both Esther and Carol were praying that God would keep their husbands safe and that they would find everything that was needed.

It was 8:00 A. M. when the train pulled out of Miles City heading for Rapid City. The 250 mile trip would take close to nine hours. As Sam watched the scenery go by, he thought about the task ahead. They planned to buy one Hereford bull and one Longhorn bull. Those would be shipped back to the ranches. Then they would buy forty heifers—some Longhorn and some Hereford—and hire some cowboys to help drive them home. Thinking about the cost of cattle, and how much cash he and Tom were carrying, Sam instinctively reached for the money belt that was around his waist.

The train pulled into Rapid City around 5:00 that afternoon. Sam was surprised to see how much the town had grown since he had been there. They got two hotel rooms and then went to see the local sheriff. He gave them directions to all the ranches that sold cattle within fifty miles of town.

"This could take a long time," Tom said, looking at the list. "With the Lord's help, we'll get it done."

The next morning, after praying for wisdom, they rented two horses and began their search. It was easy to find the forty heifers and Longhorn. On Sunday, they went to church. It was wonderful to let go of the burdens and cares of life and enjoy the wonderful services. Monday, they set off again. At the second ranch, they found a bull.

"He looks pretty good," Sam said.

"Yeah, he's a fine animal," the owner told them. He quoted them a price.

"Well, let us think about it," Sam said. He and Tom headed toward their horses.

"What do you think?" Sam asked.

"No," Tom said.

Sam was taken aback. "What?"

"Sam, he's nice, but way too expensive. Also, he doesn't have all the qualities that Mr. Holte said we should look for."

Sam was exasperated. "True, but Tom, we've looked all over for a bull, and this is the only halfway decent one we can find."

"I know, but I still say no. Let's look around the rest of the day at least. Then we'll decide."

Sam sighed. "Alright."

They hunted the rest of the morning and all afternoon, and not another good bull was to be found.

Late in the day, after leaving yet another ranch, Sam looked at Tom. "What now?"

"There's one more ranch not too far from here. Let's check it out."

Sam wanted to argue, but he held his tongue. "Okay, let's go."

The ranch house and the barn were rather small. As they rode in, Sam shook his head. He was sure they would find no prize bull here.

An elderly man stepped out onto the porch. Aided by a bamboo cane, he slowly made his way to the railing.

"Howdy," Tom called out. "I hear tell you've got cattle for sale. We're looking for a Hereford bull."

"Yes," the man said, "I've got a few cows, and I've got a bull. Right this way, boys."

It took him some time to get down off the porch. Then the three of them set off toward the barn at a slow pace. Striking up a conversation with the man, Tom found out that he was a Christian. Tom told him about their ranches in Montana.

Sam was tired and his patience was growing thin. As he fell in behind the man, he began to think about where else he could have been right then. By that time, they could have bought that other bull, made all the arrangements to ship him, hired a few hands to help drive the rest home, and had supper. Instead, they were in the middle of nowhere on a wild goose chase.

"It's nice to have folks over," the man was saying. "Why just a few moments ago I was a praying and asking the Good Lord to send someone by. Never did I imagine, He'd send folks from another state. My wife and me have no children nearby and we get a might lonely at times."

Sam looked toward the sky. Was God really answering this man's prayer by sending them?

They finally reached the barn. Once inside, Sam was surprised to see several fine Herefords.

"I've been working with cattle for, oh, about fifty years now, I reckon," the elderly man said as he led them to the back of the barn. "Seen several a fine animal in my day. This feller I've got ain't the best'n I've ever had, but he's a pretty good'un."

A partition separated one end of the barn from the rest of the building. In the middle of the partition, was a door. Their host opened it, and they entered a spacious stall.

Sam could not believe his eyes. In the middle of the stall, stood a bull. Everything Randall Holte had said about Hereford bulls was running through his mind. The animal was the right height and weight. Across the chest, he was wide and muscular. His back and the outside of his legs were reddish brown. His face, chest, belly, and inner legs were white. Everything seemed to fit.

"What is the price?" Tom asked. His heart was racing.

"Well, me and the wife are getting up in years. Don't spect we'll be working with cattle much longer, least not full time anyways. And the Lord's been mighty good to us financially. So, seein' how you boys is needin' a bull, I'll let him go for four hundred dollars."

Sam and Tom were at a loss for words. The price was a steal for such a fine bull. Finally, Sam managed to say, "It's a deal, and thank you, sir."

"You're welcome. Won't you stay to supper?"

"We'd be glad to."

Sam and Tom were not sure who enjoyed the evening more, them or the elderly couple. The man was a genius when it came to cattle and gave them a lot of information.

Before they went to their rooms that night, Sam said, "Tommy, I'm sorry I got so upset today."

Tom grinned. "That's okay. I was getting a might upset myself, but God had it all worked out."

Sam nodded. "We just got to learn to trust Him and know that whatever He does is right. That first bull was not right for us, and I knew it, even though I wanted to buy him. We would have had to get another bull, and we would have wasted money. God's way was better."

"Yeah, like Romans 8:28 says, 'And we know that all things work together for good to them that love God, to them who are the called according to his purpose.'"

Chapter 22

Foremen and Brands

By early the next day, Sam and Tom had hired ten riders to help them herd the cattle to the ranches. The two bulls would be shipped later and would arrive in Miles City after Sam and Tom got home.

As they were making their way to the corral where their stock was penned up, they heard a familiar voice.

"Sam! Tom! Wait up!"

They looked back and were surprised to find Ralf Raff and Clint, two young cowboys who had come west on the wagon train with them.

"Well, what do you know!" Tom exclaimed.

"What are you two doing down here?" Sam asked.

"Once we got to Montana, we started looking for work," Ralf explained. "Ended up joining a big trail herd driving a few thousand head to the railroads down here in the

Dakotas. When we got here, we kept finding work, so we stayed."

Sam and Tom glanced at each other. "Are you working right now?" Sam asked.

"We were working for an elderly gentleman whose ranch was about done in. He decided to go back east, so, no, we don't have a job."

"Want one?" Tom enquired.

"Sure do," Ralf answered.

"You've got one," Sam told them. "The Lord blessed Tom and me with a great piece of land. We came down here to buy cattle. In about an hour, we'll be driving forty heifers back to our ranch, and you're welcome to come along."

Raff and Clint smiled. "You've got a deal," Raff said.

It was Sam and Tom's first real trail drive. They were glad Raff and Clint were there to give them some instructions.

"Sam," Tom began on the second day of the trip, "you and I don't know much about cattle."

"You can say that again," Sam concurred. Already, he had nearly lost two cows. If some cowhands had not been there, they would have escaped into the brush.

"Well, I've been watching Ralf. That boy knows cattle. What about hiring him as—"

"Foreman," Sam finished for him. "I've been thinking the same thing, but Clint's just as good."

"Yeah, I know. That's one thing that bothers me. Which one should we hire?"

"Let's pray about it."

The days passed by ever so slowly. Finally, Friday came and they would be home in a few days. It was then that God answered their prayers.

Ralf and Tom were scouting ahead and Clint and Sam were riding left flank.

"What all have you done since you reached Miles City?" Sam asked.

Clint, who rarely said much unless it was important, answered in his slow, pleasant way. "Ralf and I decided to stay together. We worked on a couple of spreads, but couldn't find one that needed full-time hands. So, we drifted until we found that elderly man who had a ranch about four miles from Rapid City. He needed help. He and his wife were real sweet people. Ralf became foreman. I'm glad it was him and not me, because I ain't cut out to be in charge. He called me his assistant foreman."

He chuckled. "It all amounted to nothing but title. We were the only two hands there, but it was great. Ralf's become like a brother, and I enjoyed working under him."

Sam's eyes lit up. Ralf would be their foreman and Clint would be second foreman.

That night Sam and Tom approached the two young men with the plan.

"That would be great!" Ralf exclaimed. Clint smiled and nodded.

The drive took eleven days. Mike and Mac were playing in a tree behind the house when MacShane saw the cattle coming.

"Hey look, Tommy!" Mac said. Sometimes the twins called each other by their middle names, Thomas and Tyler. "Is that a bunch of cows coming?" he asked, peering around a limb.

Mike looked and shouted with delight. "Yeah, it's Dad and Uncle Tom! They're bringing the cows! Come on, Ty, let's go tell the others."

The twins made their way down the tree and sprinted to the house. They burst through the door and yelled, "Dad's home!"

The family ran outside.

"Look at all the cows," Martin said.

"We're going to be cowboys!" Montana exclaimed, jumping up and down.

"You sure are," Esther laughed as she hugged him.

"This is wonderful," Carol whispered. "I've been dreaming of this day for years."

"Me, too," Esther agreed.

Matthew was grinning from ear to ear. He took hold of his mother's hand and squeezed it. She squeezed back.

Sam, Tom, and the ranch hands put the cattle in the spacious corral made for the occasion. After the cattle were secured, Sam and Tom ran to see their families.

"Welcome home, cowboy." Carol threw her arms around her husband.

Esther's eyes brimmed with tears as she welcomed Sam.

It was an important day for the two families. Their ranches had cattle and a foreman, and were becoming real working ranches.

Within a few days, the two bulls arrived. When Ralf and Clint brought them home, everyone was excited.

"They're beautiful!" Carol exclaimed. "Absolutely beautiful!"

"Oh, yes," Esther agreed. "Are we going to name them?"

"I think it would be appropriate," Sam said. "You and Carol name them."

"You pick the one you want to name, Esther," Carol said. Esther knew Carol wanted to name the Hereford, and she was glad, for she liked the Longhorn.

"I choose the Texas Longhorn, and I'm going to name him Diotrephes."

"What?" Matthew asked.

"Diotrephes. You'll find him in the book of Third John. John says that Diotrephes 'loveth to have the preeminence among them,' I get the feeling that this boy will have the preeminence."

The others laughed and agreed.

"Your turn, Carol," Tom said.

"Caesar," she said without hesitation.

"Caesar and Diotrephes," Tom repeated. "That's great."

They divided the forty heifers into two groups of twenty, putting Diotrephes with half in the west pasture and Caesar with half in the east pasture.

The men Sam and Tom had hired decided to stay on as permanent hands. The two owners were glad, for the men seemed dependable.

The next day, Mike stood in front of his father's desk with a piece of paper hid behind his back.

"Dad?"

Sam laid aside his paperwork and smiled. "Yes, Professor."

"Well, I was wondering. Brother Holte said that every rancher needs a brand. Since we've got some cattle, I thought maybe we could get a brand."

"Is that what you've got behind your back?"

"Yes, sir." He handed the paper to his father.

Sam leaned forward and looked at it. The design for their ranch was the letter *S* with an arrow through it, a simple yet neat design. The one for Tom's ranch amazed Sam. It was a wing with an *M* in the center. Lines extending from the top and bottom of the *M* attached it to the edges of the wing.

"These are really good, Mikey. I'll show them to Uncle Tom and see what he thinks."

Mike grinned. "Thanks, Dad."

Sam chuckled as he watched his son run from the room. Sam had an idea, and if Tom consented, he would get to work on it right away.

On Saturday, Eight-year-old Matthew, astride a Mustang mare he called Cookie, watched the cattle grazing in the pasture below. His father, mounted on Sunny, was beside him.

"Dad, look at that cow down there. Is she limping?"

Sam followed his son's gaze and watched the cow. Sure enough, she had a slight limp.

"You got good eyesight, Warrior. I'd have never noticed her limping without you showing me."

Sam headed his horse down the hill. He and one of the hands cut the cow out of the herd and examined her leg. It was only a scratch. After applying ointment to the leg, they let her back in the herd. Caesar watched but paid them no mind. He was friendly, unlike the rowdy Diotrephes. All of Sam's boys liked Caesar, but Esther preferred the Longhorn and, surprisingly, Diotrephes liked her. She could walk right up to him and he would let her pet him. She always brought him a special treat, and he would take it from her gently.

Sam rode back to where Matthew was waiting and they rode home.

"It won't be too long before some calves are born, right, Dad?"

"By next spring, we should have a handful of them at least, the Lord willing."

"I can't wait."

As they rode in silence, Sam thought about his oldest son. Sitting tall and straight in the saddle, Matthew held the reins securely in his hands and was in full control of the horse. Sam knew he was going to be tall, because he was already taller than Sam had been at his age. Wise beyond his years, he seemed grown-up. Though he liked to play as much as any other boy, he had a grown-up's personality. He took on responsibility and he was trustworthy. Even at eight years old, he did more than his share around the ranch, and he enjoyed it. Matt liked to watch and listen to people, especially concerning ranching. He loved to sit in the study while Sam and Tom went over ranch business and to read books and magazines about ranching, horses, and cattle. Already, he had enough knowledge to work well on a spread. He still had a lot of learning to do, but he was teachable.

They reached the house just in time for supper. The Sampsons were eating dinner with them. Sam caught Tom's eye. Tom nodded.

Good, Sam thought to himself. *Praise the Lord. I can hardly wait.*

After dinner was over, Sam told everyone that he and Tom had a surprise for them. Tom jumped out of his seat and ran from the room.

"What is it, Dad?" Mac asked.

"You'll have to wait and see."

"Is anyone peeking?" Tom called.

"No," Sam said.

Tom tiptoed in with a box in each hand. He gave one to Sam. Paper rustled as they unwrapped the packages.

"All right everyone," Tom said eagerly. "You can open your eyes."

The seven people sitting at the table gasped in delight, especially Mike. Each man held a branding iron for their ranch. The brands were exactly the way Mike had drawn them.

Mike jumped out of his chair and ran to his dad's side. "You used them!" he exclaimed.

Sam smiled and let him hold the brand in his small hands.

"Wow, it's heavy," he said.

"They're great, Dad, Uncle Tom," Matthew said.

Esther and Carol inspected the brands along with the others. "Did Murphy make them?" Esther asked, noting the fine work that was typical of the blacksmith.

"Yeah, he did," Sam answered.

"He did great," Carol said. "I really like the brand for our ranch."

"Mike designed them both," Tom said.

"Really?" the others chorused.

"You did a great job," Esther praised him.

"He sure did," Carol agreed.

"When can we use them?" Montana asked as he ran his hand over the metal arrow.

"Monday," Tom said. "Monday we'll begin the branding."

The next two days were spent branding their small herd. After the last cow was branded, the families looked joyfully at the herd that bore their marks.

Since the work was over, the punchers were resting their weary horses. Matthew, with Montana at his side, stood by the dying fire and watched the cowboys care for their mounts. Esther and Carol were resting on the buckboard. Martin had fallen asleep in his mother's arms and Duke, worn out from helping cut the cattle, was stretched out at Esther's feet. Ralf and Clint were playing cowboys and Indians with the twins with one man and one boy on each side. Battle stations were on either side of the chuck wagon.

"God is so good," Tom said, enjoying the moment. He and Sam had loosened the cinches on their saddles and were watering their horses.

Sam nodded. "Look," he said, pointing to a ridge in the distance.

It took Tom a moment to see the three deer. Camouflaged in the trees, they grazed serenely and contentedly.

His eyes sweeping over the vast land, Tom suddenly straightened. "Look, an eagle!"

"I see him," Sam said breathlessly. "Another one of God's blessings. It may seem small to others, but it shows His love just as much as the homes and herds of cattle He has given us. We have a great God."

Chapter 23

Esther's Bull

Esther and Carol were preparing supper one evening when Carol gasped in surprise.

"What is it?" Esther asked.

"I can't believe how fast the time has gone. This August will be two years that we've been in Montana!"

Esther stopped kneading her bread. "Two years. That's amazing. The boys will be nine, eight, seven, and six."

"*Also*," Carol added, "this June is our tenth wedding anniversary."

"My, my," Esther whispered. "Ten wonderful years."

"Yes."

Carol finished cutting up the carrots before asking, "Did you see how big Tom's colt is getting?"

"Yes, I saw Tom working with him. How is the training coming?"

"Wonderful," Carol smiled. "Tom really likes that horse."

"He named him Jehu, didn't he?"

"Yes. In the Old Testament, Jehu was a man who drove furiously. So Tommy named the colt Jehu, because he's so fast."

They heard Montana playing the piano and both were amazed at how well he was doing. His mother gave him lessons, and he loved them. He spent hours on the piano and Esther could tell that God had blessed her son with musical ability.

The first Monday in April was about to slip away when there came a pounding on Sam's door. Since Duke was not growling, Sam knew the person outside was a friend. When he opened the door, Clint was there, short of breath.

"It's . . . Diotrephes," he panted, and pointed to the barn.

Standing behind her husband, Esther gasped. They hurried to the barn. Clint stayed in the house in case the boys woke up.

Ralf had the Longhorn in the box stall. Blood flowed from deep gashes that covered his speckled body.

Sam knelt beside the bull. "What happened?"

"Wolves tried to get to one of the cows. This boy took care of them, but . . ." he sighed.

"How bad is it?" Esther asked.

"Pretty bad, ma'am," Ralf answered.

Esther knelt and examined the wounds. "Can we try to help him?"

Sam looked at Ralf. "What do you think, Ralf?"

He shrugged. "Not much hope, but we'll give it a try."

For a week, the three of them tended the injured bull. The wounds were cleaned and bandaged. Esther closed some of the cuts with stitches, but the bull did not get better.

When the week had gone by, Sam decided it best to put him down. *Tomorrow morning*, he thought to himself. *If he's not better, we'll put him out of his misery*. He glanced at Esther. She carefully checked the wounds and then began to stroke the massive head. Sam sighed. He would tell her the next morning.

That night, Esther and Sam took turns sitting with the bull. Esther wanted the first watch, so Sam stretched out on the barn floor and fell asleep.

The minutes passed slowly for Esther. How she wished he could get better. Then a thought struck her. *Not once have I prayed for this animal. Does God care whether or not this bull lives?* In answer to her question, verses crowded into her mind. *"Delight thyself also in the LORD; and he shall give thee the desires of thine heart. . . . Ask, and it shall be given you; seek, and ye shall find; knock, and it shall be opened unto you:. . . . ye have not, because ye ask not. . . . For with God nothing shall be impossible. . . . Casting all your care upon him; for he careth for you. . . . there is nothing too hard for thee:"* She lifted her eyes toward the ceiling and began to pray. "Dear God, You know how special this bull is. I pray that You would raise him up. I do want Your will to be done, and if it's not Your will, then I accept that. If You see fit, please heal Diotrephes."

Early that morning, as Esther was taking her second watch, the bull began to stir. For the first time in many days, he lifted his giant head.

"Sam!" she called. "Sam, look!"

Her husband jumped to his feet and hurried to her side. They watched in wonder as the

Longhorn once again lifted his head and looked around.

"Let's see if he can eat on his own," Sam said. They had been feeding him through a long rubber tube. This time, as Sam helped hold his head up and Esther placed the bucket of soft mash close to his mouth, he began to feed. They held the water bucket up to him and he drank deeply.

"I'm gonna get Ralf and see what he thinks," Sam said. Before he left, he gave Esther a hug.

Ralf and Clint came running into the barn and stopped at the sight of the bull. The spark was back in his eyes, and he even let out a weak, "Moooo."

"I don't believe it!" Ralf fairly shouted.

Sam glanced at Esther. "You prayed, didn't you?"

She smiled. "'Ye have not, because ye ask not.' God raised him up."

Three days later, Diotrephes tried to stand, but he was weak and sunk back down.

Sam, Tom, their wives, and Clint and Ralf were watching.

"Can't we try to help him?" Esther asked.

"No, ma'am," Ralf answered. "He's way too big for us to move and it would be too easy for him to come down on top of one of us. I'm sorry."

Sam put his arm around Esther. It was all they could do to watch the great animal struggle.

"Please, God," Carol whispered. "Please help him up."

Twice more the bull failed, but on the third try he stood up. The onlookers held their breath. Would he be able to stay on his feet?

Swaying some from lack of strength, the bull looked around. He saw Esther and took a wobbly step toward her.

Ralf grinned. "I think he'll be alright." He opened the stall door and motioned for Esther to come in. Esther, blinking back tears, came up to him and began to pet him. He licked her hand.

"Thank You, Lord," they all chorused.

Soon, Diotrephes returned to his herd.

Mac and his mother went for a ride to see the bull. He looked fit and had gained back some weight. He stood away from the other cattle, watching carefully and occasionally tossing his head as if to dare anyone to mess with his herd.

"Momma, did God heal Diotrephes?" Mac asked.

"Yes, He did."

MacShane looked at the bull again before asking, "So, God can do anything right?"

"Yes, dear, He can."

"Momma, is it okay then to pray that the deer I saw limping the other day would be alright?"

Esther turned to face him. "Yes, son. God cares about the things that are dear to your heart. Always remember that He loves you and He wants you to share all your burdens with Him, even the ones that others think are not important."

Chapter 24

Winds of Change

Esther watched the cattle graze on a warm May day. The air smelled sweet from the abundance of flowers and the rain that had fallen the day before. "Isn't that a beautiful sight? The very thought that in a few years we'll be shipping our cattle off to market thrills me." She began to pet the chestnut mare she was riding.

"God is good," Sam agreed.

After checking on the other herd, they turned toward home.

Esther slowed her horse to take in all the sights. "I love this place. I'm glad we came here."

Sam smiled. "Not this August, but the next, will be Matthew's tenth birthday. Remember, I wanted to get each of the boys a horse all their own when they turned ten?"

"I do remember. Matthew will be so happy." She sighed. "Martin worries me sometimes.

He's so headstrong. I fear that if he's not saved at an early age, he will live a wild life."

Sam agreed. He had also been thinking about their youngest son. "Let's pray for him right now," he suggested. They stopped their horses, dismounted, and knelt on the grassy slope.

"Dear Lord," Sam began, "how thankful we are for this wonderful place, for our family and friends. Lord, our hearts are heavy for Marty. Please speak to him and draw him to You. Thank You that the other boys have trusted You as their Saviour. Amen."

"Lord," Esther added, "I pray that both Sam and I will live to see our last son get saved. Amen."

Sam and Esther mounted, and then went on their way. They had no idea that soon Esther's prayer would become very important.

On June 1, six days before their wedding anniversaries, Tom was trying to decide what to get Carol.

"Hey, Sam, what are you getting Esther?" he whispered as they were cleaning out the stalls in the barn.

Sam looked at Tom in bewilderment. "Tommy, it's not her birthday."

Tom laughed. "Sam, you've lost track of time. June seventh is coming up."

Sam was still confused.

"Our tenth wedding anniversary," Tom explained. "Remember, I married a girl named Carol that day, and you married a girl named Esther?" he added teasingly.

Sam shook his head. "Am I ever glad you reminded me. I have no idea what to get her but I better think of something right quick."

They prayed, talked, and planned, but no good ideas came to mind.

The next day, Tom received a telegram. After paying the lad who delivered it, Tom opened the envelope and read the short note. He nearly shouted. He ran outside, grabbing his hat on the way. In just a few minutes, he had saddled his horse and headed toward the Silver Arrow. Much to his surprise, Sam met him on the way.

"I got a telegram!" they both yelled. "So did I," they answered together.

Tom, laughing at the confusion, held up his hand for silence. "You go first."

"I got a telegram from Esther's parents. They're coming up for our wedding anniversary."

"So are Carol's parents," Tom said. "What a great surprise for the girls."

The men, trying to be inconspicuous, spent the next few days getting things ready. What they did not know was that Esther and Carol were doing the same thing for they had received telegrams from their husbands' parents saying that they, too, were coming.

On June 7 the two couples left the boys to spend the day with the Holtes and headed to town to celebrate. Sam and Esther were each trying to conceal their excitement that the children were going to see their grandparents again that evening.

As they traveled, the men exchanged glances as the ladies talked about the nice dinner they were going to have in town. Esther and Carol hid their smiles as the men hinted at the fun that was in store for the day.

"Look, the train is coming," Tom said after getting out of the wagon. Most people in town were still thrilled over the railroad extending to Miles City and many made a habit to watch the train pull in and see what kind of people were on it.

"Let's meet it," Carol suggested.

"That'll be fine," Sam said. He took Esther's hand and headed for the station. If he had not been so thrilled himself, he might have felt Esther squeeze his hand more tightly than normal.

The train pulled in and passengers began to disembark. One by one they came, but none were familiar. When it seemed that the last ones were stepping off, the two couples were downhearted. They turned away and started back toward the main part of town wondering what could have happened to their family.

"Surprise!"

They whirled around to see dozens of smiling faces. Everyone was there. Josh and Mary Goodton, Joel and Virginia Sampson, Laramie and Lisa Maker, and Henry and Susie Grey were there, and there were more. Sam's brother Tyler, his wife Cecilia, and their two children Ellen and Archibald were there. Shane Glenmaker jumped out of the car and ran to embrace Esther. The four Indian girls that the Greys had adopted were next, with Melissa, her husband Joah, and their two-month-old boy in the lead. Leah and Tiffany were right behind them. An Indian boy that

Carol did not recognize helped Jane down.
This was Jane's husband that Carol had heard
much about. Finally, Carol's birth sister Tessa,
her husband Todd, and their triplets got off the
train.

Sam, Esther, Tom, and Carol were too
moved for words. They cried and hugged and
hugged and cried for twenty minutes. It all
seemed like a dream. Eventually, they were
able to get everyone's luggage loaded into
rented buckboards.

Soon, they were at the Silver Arrow. The
boys were happy to see their families.
Montana and Martin had been very young
when they came out west and did not
remember some of them. They ran from one
person to another asking, "Who are you?" It
was grand.

Things had definitely changed since the two
young couples had moved from Indiana. Joel
Sampson was slowly being crippled by arthritis.
He and Virginia were going to sell their half of
the farm and move in with Joshua and Mary
Goodton. The Greys had started an
orphanage under the authority of the Clear
Water Baptist Church. The Makers worked
with them. Joah, Melissa, Jane, and her

husband Ken had started churches on five different reservations in Florida and Georgia. Leah and Tiffany worked in the orphanage and loved it. Both, of them, were engaged. Todd owned the largest shipping industry in Maine. Most men who achieved such wealth no longer personally sailed, preferring to send reliable captains in their place, but not Todd. He still treasured the sea. Quite often, he would put away his captain's uniform and be there amongst the crew, wearing the striped shirt and pants of a sailor.

The visitors stayed for eight days. The younger Goodtons and Sampsons rejoiced at being able to show them all that the Lord had done for them in Montana. One day, they all went to Miles City and had the town photographer take their picture.

During the week, they showed them life around the ranch. Joel and Josh watched in admiration as Sam and Tom showed them what ranch work was like.

The Makers and Greys spent time with their daughters. Esther and Carol showed them the new kinds of flowers and birds that they had come to love.

Matthew and his brothers played themselves exhausted with their two cousins, Ellen and Archie. Todd's girls were welcomed into the circle of friends. Duke had a time with ten kids to play with.

Sam and Tom took Todd on a miniature roundup. He was awkward with cattle at first, but soon had the hang of it.

Carol was elated to have her five sisters with her. They talked for hours about things that had happened in the past few years. Jane was expecting her first child.

Esther cherished having Shane there. After supper, he would play with the boys until bedtime. Then the brother and sister would visit long into the night with their mom and dad.

Joah and Ken enjoyed the fellowship with other Christian men. Many of the men in the churches they had started were new Christians and did not know much about the Bible so it was refreshing to be around other men who knew the Bible and enjoyed talking about it.

It was good to hear news from home. The church was growing and so were its families. Terry and Abby had three girls and one boy. Luke Neils and his wife had two boys. Tim Lard had ten children, six girls and four boys.

"How are the Pitts?" Sam asked, referring to the singing family that went to their church. Brother Pitt, his wife, and three daughters traveled to different churches and provided special music.

"They had to move to Delaware last year," Joshua said sadly. He explained that their youngest daughter, who had married a pastor in Delaware, had suffered a terrible back injury. Her parents had gone to help them care for their baby until she recovered.

The best part, for the family, was going to church together. They filled up half of one side of the building. The younger Goodtons and Sampsons were thrilled to have their family hear their preacher. They went Wednesday, all day Sunday, and the next Wednesday. On Sunday afternoon, they had a picnic on the church property like they used to back in Indiana. It brought back so many memories.

All too soon, the time was up. On June 16, they left to go back east.

The younger Goodtons and Sampsons waved goodbye until the train was out of sight.

Esther took hold of Sam's hand and leaned against him. "That was one of the most wonderful weeks, of my life."

"Mine too," Sam told her. He could not have known how special the week really was but as the years would pass, Sam would remember that week as the last week they were all together.

Winter came early that year. By the end of October, there was already two feet of snow. Sam and Tom were worried about the cattle. They were glad their herd was small, for it was easier to keep track of them. Ralf and Clint kept men watching the cattle around the clock. Hay and grain were given as liberally as possible.

They were thankful that they had built large barns, because all their horses were able to stay inside and there was room for some of the cattle that could not stand the cold. A few of their cows had given birth a week earlier. All of them were in the barn.

"If this keeps up . . ." Sam did not finish the sentence. He pulled the door shut and glanced at Esther. She wanted to ask how everything was, but she waited. He would tell her in time.

"I'm sorry, Esther. I know God's in control and, really, things aren't bad. I just feel like we're barely keeping ahead of catastrophe."

"Remember, Sam, 'Casting all your care upon him; for he careth for you.'"

Sam hugged her. "I love you, Esther honey."

December came and the weather grew colder. Esther was adding more wood to the fire when she heard a strange noise coming from the barn. Worried, she called for Matthew.

He hurried to her side, "Yes, ma'am."

"Matthew, something's going on in the barn. Dad and Uncle Tom are gone, so I'll check on it. Keep the boys inside, no matter what." She opened the gun cabinet and handed him a rifle. "You know how to use this. Keep it close in case it's a wild animal, and stay inside with Duke." In her haste to insure everyone's safety, she grabbed only a light shawl before taking another rifle out of the gun case. Sam had bought the Winchester for her on her last birthday, and Esther was a good shot. She made sure it was loaded and stepped outside.

The snow so thick she could barely see, Esther took hold of the rope that spanned the distance between the house and barn. Once she reached the barn door, she pressed her ear against the wood. It sounded as though a cow and calf were bawling. She raised the rifle to her shoulder and pushed open the door. When nothing of immediate danger met her arrival, she peeked inside.

A calf, one they had named Augustus, was caught in something. Quickly, Esther tied up the mother in another stall to keep her from interfering and went to the calf's aide.

His hoof was stuck in a small hole in the side of the stall. Esther worked for ten minutes to free the fragile leg. It was difficult, because her gloveless hands were numb from the cold. When the calf was loose, Esther applied ointment and a bandage to the leg. Then, finding a board, some nails, and a hammer, she covered up the hole before letting the mother back in the stall. The calf must have been caught for some time, for he immediately began to nurse once his mother joined him.

"Poor thing," Esther said. "You were hungry."

Esther spent another half hour checking the other animals before going back inside.

"What was it, Mom?" Matthew asked. Then he saw how she was shivering. "Are you okay?"

Esther realized how cold she really was. "Yes, I think I'm just cold. The noise we heard was only a calf."

The snow let up enough to allow Sam to get back home, but no sooner had he put up his horse than the storms started again.

The next day, Esther awoke with a tightness in her chest. She coughed so much and so hard that her ribcage was sore.

Sam was already up and checking the stock. When he came in, he was surprised to see that Esther was not in the kitchen. *Maybe she's still resting*, he thought. *I won't wake her up.* Then he heard her cough. The very sound was chilling. With Duke at his heels, he ran up the stairs and into the bedroom. She was shivering.

"Esther, are you alright?"

"Sam, oh Sam, I feel sick."

"What's wrong?" he asked, panic rising inside him.

"My chest hurts. I can't quit coughing, and I can't breathe very well. Oh, I'm so cold."

He felt her forehead. "Esther, you have a fever. Lie back down." Once he had helped her back into bed and covered her with several blankets, Sam quickly got a wet washcloth and bathed her face.

The weather was too bad to go for a doctor. He could not even go get Carol. The snow was so thick that he could see no more than a few inches in front of him. All the ranch hands were bunked at the Meadowlark. Sam and his family were alone, and he felt that there was nothing else he could do. Then he remembered Esther's verse: "Casting all your care upon him; for he careth for you."

"Oh, Lord," Sam prayed, "help us."

As the storm raged, Esther grew worse. Her fever went up and she became delirious.

Sam paced the floor, sat beside the bed, paced again, checked on the boys, then went back to his wife's side. Once he nearly decided to try for the Meadowlark, thinking that maybe Duke could lead the way, but he thought of what would happen if Esther passed away while he was gone. The boys would be there all alone. He could not leave them. Besides, there was no way he could reach Tom's house. He would have to wait.

For three long days he waited. Finally, on Saturday the weather cleared.

Immediately, Sam went for help. He made it to Tom's house, and Tommy and Carol came to Esther's aid.

Clint volunteered to go for the doctor, but Sam did not want the young cowboy to get caught in a snowstorm. When he expressed his worry, Clint reassured him.

"Don't worry about me, Boss. God will help me." Soon he was braving the cold and the threat of more storms to bring help for Esther. It took awhile, but he returned with the doctor.

"Esther has pneumonia," Dr. James said. "It's pretty bad, but there is hope. Just a few months ago I received a supply of medicine to treat this. I've given her some and also some medicine to bring the fever down."

"What can we do?" Carol asked.

"Here's a chart that will tell you when to give her the medicine. Every four hours she gets one pill and every eight hours give her this liquid. Keep applying the cool compresses, and try to make her comfortable."

The doctor spent the rest of the day there, and then Clint escorted him back to town.

The medicine worked quickly. Two days later, Esther awoke from her fever.

Chapter 25

A Strange Request

Esther, though it seemed she was no longer in danger, could not get completely well. She still had coughing spells and had very little strength. After doing small household tasks, she had to rest. Her boys were quick to lend her a hand, and Tom took over much of the ranch work, leaving Sam to care for her. In spite of the illness, Esther's personality did not change. She was still happy and peaceful.

March brought an early spring and everything began to bloom at once. Work doubled on the ranches with crops to be planted and cattle checked and branded. Colts needed gentling, and it seemed that every mare they had was about to foal.

Esther viewed the activity from the window. The wind blew strongly at times, so it was too cold for her to be outside much. A tear trickled down her cheek as she watched a few hands head for the cattle herds. She longed to be out in the garden or lending a hand with the branding, but whenever she felt frustrated at being inside, she would think of Romans 8:28: "And we know that all things work together for good to them that love God, to them who are the called according to his purpose."

"God has a reason," she reminded herself. "At least we've been able to go to church." The whole family loved to go to church. Pastor McBride always preached messages that helped them, and their church family had been supportive during Esther's illness. She was thankful most of all for their prayers.

She began to feel tired and went to lie down. Pulling a blanket over herself, she turned her eyes to the flower sitting on her windowsill. It was the bitterroot Matthew named "Hope." Esther had planned to put it in the garden but it thrived so well in the house that she changed her mind. Though it probably would not bloom until sometime late April or early May, Sam had put it in their room so Esther could enjoy it when it when it did bloom.

She fingered the floral design on her blouse. The clock showed that it was close to lunchtime. Sam would be home soon and the family would eat together. Matthew had started cooking the noon meal, and he did a fine job. The food was tasty, and he always cleaned up after himself.

The door opened and Sam stepped in. "You have company, Esther."

She sat up as he approached her and wrapped a heavy shawl around her. He then lifted her into his arms.

"Sam," she protested. "Let me at least fix my hair."

"Oh, I don't think your company will mind if your hair is not done."

He carried her down the stairs and through the living room. Montana, waiting for them, opened the front door.

When they stepped onto the porch they were greeted by a loud "MOOOOO."

"Diotrephes!" Esther exclaimed.

Sam let her stand next to the bull. Esther rubbed his face and his eyes closed in delight.

"He threatened to stampede the whole herd unless we brought him over to see you," Tom said with a grin.

Esther laughed. The sun felt good on her face and the air smelled fresh and clean. Mike handed her a carrot that she gave to the bull. He munched on it and then licked her hand.

"Thank you, Mike," she said before turning to her husband. "And thank you, Sam."

"You're welcome, Esther honey." He drew her close to him. With a contented sigh, she leaned against his broad shoulder.

The days went by, yet Esther did not fully recover. Carol came over every day to help her with the housework, especially the ironing, a chore that really wore Esther out.

Carol knocked once to announce her coming. She waited a second and then stepped inside. Esther was sitting on the couch knitting. Duke was at her side.

"Good afternoon, Carol."

"Good afternoon, Esther." Carol hugged her friend. "My, you look better today. I do believe some color is coming back into your cheeks."

"I feel quite well today."

"I'm glad. If you don't mind, I'll fix us some tea." She stepped into the kitchen and filled the teapot with water. After setting it on the stove, she checked the washroom to see how much ironing there was. She was surprised to find the laundry basket empty. She felt the stove and iron. They were both warm. She returned to the living room.

"Esther, did you do the ironing?"

"No, Sam did it for me."

"Oh," Carol said, turning back to the kitchen. "Wait a minute." She turned to face her friend. "Did you say *Sam* did your ironing?"

"Yes. He set up a chair for me in the washroom and we talked while he ironed." She smiled. "We had a good time just talking about all the wonderful blessings God has sent us."

From then on it became tradition. Sam bought a small couch and put it in the washroom for Esther to sit or lay on. Every Monday, he would iron as they prayed and talked.

"What are you knitting, Esther?" Carol asked one morning. It was the first day of June.

"A baby blanket."

"Really? For who?" Carol's face lit up at the thought of new life.

"Someone we both know is going to have a baby, I think."

"How wonderful! Who is it?"

"I can't tell you now, but I think you'll find out soon," Esther said, not looking at her needles as she started the next row.

Carol studied Esther for a few seconds. "Esther, are you . . . ?"

"No, not me." Although she would have loved to have more, the doctor had told them after Martin was born that she should not. "No, it's someone else."

"You said I know her?"

"Yes."

"Then who . . . ?"

"I can't tell you, because I don't know for certain. However, I'm pretty sure that I'm right." Esther stopped her knitting and reached for Carol's hand. "Carol, it would mean a lot to this person if *you* would make her a blanket, also."

Tears came to Carol's eyes and she looked down at the skirt she was hemming. "Esther, I can't. I've tried to make things for babies but I can't. It hurts too much. I know God had a reason for not sending us a child. I accept that, but I can't make . . . make things like . . . like that."

Esther laid aside her knitting and hugged her. "I know it's hard, Carol, but," she sat back and looked into her friend's eyes, "will you try?" She wiped a tear from Carol's cheek.

"Is it really that important?" When Esther nodded, Carol sighed. "Alright, I'll try."

Back at the Meadowlark, Carol cried for hours. "Dear God, please help me," she prayed. "I don't know if I can do this, but Esther wants me to. I don't want to let her down, but it's so hard." Carol saw her Bible lying on the dresser and she picked it up. Hands trembling, she turned to the book of Matthew. She began reading in chapter one. When she got to verse eighteen, the verses seem to jump from the pages and grab her heart.

> "Now the birth of Jesus Christ was on this wise: When as his mother Mary was espoused to Joseph, before they came together, she was found with child of the Holy Ghost.
>
> "Then Joseph her husband, being a just man, and not willing to make her a publick example, was minded to put her away privily.
>
> "But while he thought on these things, behold, the angel of the Lord appeared unto him in a dream, saying, Joseph, thou son of David, fear not to take unto thee

Mary thy wife: for that which is conceived in her is of the Holy Ghost.

"And she shall bring forth a son, and thou shalt call his name JESUS: for he shall save his people from their sins."

When she read the last verse in the passage, she paused. A phrase from Hebrews came to her memory: "and without shedding of blood is no remission."

"Jesus was born to die," Carol said aloud. She already knew that, but the truth somehow became clearer. "Born to die, for *my* sins and for the sins of the whole world." Her mind went to the day Jesus was baptized, when God's voice was heard, saying, "This is my beloved Son, in whom I am well pleased." She pondered how God could allow His only Son Whom He dearly loved to come down to earth and die for the sins of men.

"Dear Father," she whispered, "how much You love us. You allowed Your Son to die to purchase my salvation. Then You offer the gift of salvation to all men freely. All we must do is call and ask for this gift. Lord, if I had a child, I don't know if I could give them up for someone else, even for a friend. You did though, and for

Your enemies. So, since You were willing to do all that just because You love me, I can rest knowing You are working something out in this situation. I can't understand why I have no children. I can't understand why Esther wants me to make this blanket, but I know that You love me and that You told Paul, 'My grace is sufficient for thee:' I know that Your grace is sufficient. Thank You, Lord."

Carol stood up and dried her eyes. She took two knitting needles and a ball of soft white yarn. Praying for help, she began to knit.

When Tom came home for supper, Carol was cooking and knitting at the same time.

"Did you run out of dishcloths and hot pads trying to make this meal?" he teased.

She hugged him, her face beaming radiantly. "Oh, Tom," she said, "you'll never believe what has happened." They sat down, and after telling him the story she said, "I've been knitting all afternoon, and the Lord is helping me to actually enjoy it. I've been praying for this mother and baby and such a peace has come over me. I did cry, even after I read the Bible, and I still hurt a little, but not like before."

With a lump in his throat, Tom reached for her hands. "I'm glad, Carol, very glad. I love you." He held her and they kissed.

Near the end of the month Carol had to go to the doctor. She had flu-like symptoms and Tom was worried that she might become deathly ill as Esther had.

After giving her a check-up, Dr. James called them both into his office.

"It's an unusual thing," he said. "Tommy, I *thought*, along with the other doctors you've seen, that your wife would never have a baby. However, I'm *sure* that your wife is . . . ," he paused and smiled, "pregnant."

Tom fainted and fell off his chair. The doctor, expecting such a reaction, had smelling salts handy. He rushed to Tom's side and waved the bottle in front his nose. A few seconds later, Tom blinked his eyes and looked up at the laughing doctor.

"Tom, get up and hug your wife," Dr. James said, pulling him to his feet.

Carol was weeping with joy. Tom wrapped his arms around her and together they praised God. The doctor, still smiling, quietly left the room.

All the way home, they rejoiced. They could not express the joy in words, but their hearts were singing God's praise.

They went home first to try to get control of their emotions. Finally Carol said, "I think I'm ready to go see Esther." She turned, and her eyes rested on the half-finished baby blanket. "Esther knew! I don't know how, but she knew."

They kissed and then held each other for a moment.

"I love you, Carol."

"I love you, too, Tommy."

Then they went to spread the good news.

Carol walked to the front door of the Silver Arrow. Tears still streaming down her cheeks, she gave her customary knock and hurried inside.

Esther was sitting on the couch waiting for her. Carol threw her arms around her and cried. Esther held her friend close and gently patted her shoulder.

"How did you know?" Carol asked, stepping back.

"It was written all over your face. Of course, I didn't know for certain, but I thought so."

Tom, meanwhile, was looking for Sam. He heard him whistling and stopped to figure out where the sound was coming from. Just then Sam came out of the barn. Tom gave a shout and tackled him in a bear hug.

"Thomas Joel Sampson, what has gotten into you?" Sam exclaimed as Tom helped him up.

"Carol . . . she's . . . doctor says he don't know how, but he said . . . oh it's wonderful . . . Carol is . . . I . . . I'm just so happy, I . . ."

Sam grabbed Tom's shoulders. "Tommy," he said slowly, "slow down. What did the doctor say?"

"We're going to have a baby!"

Sam's mouth fell open. "What!"

"A baby!"

It was Sam's turn to tackle Tom, but they managed to stay on their feet this time.

The two families hosted a party. All the ranch hands came, as well as the McBrides, the Kenneths, the Rays, Dr. James, and the Holtes. It was such a wonderful time.

The next day, Tom approached Sam with his harmonica in hand.

"Hey, that makes me think of my guitar," Sam said. "I haven't played that in a long time.

We used to play together a lot. I think I'll get it out and see if it'll still tune up."

"I haven't played in a while either. Remember this song?" He began to play a lullaby.

"Sort of. I know I've heard it before."

"It's the song I wrote. 'Member I played it for you that morning we had our first crop harvested in Indiana. I never knew what I would do with it, but now I know. It will be a lullaby for . . . for . . . for our baby." The very words choked him up.

"Have you written any words to it?"

"No, not yet, but Carol and I are going to work on it."

A few nights later, Esther and Sam sat out on the couch to talk.

"I'm so happy for Carol and Tom," Esther said.

"Me, too." Sam felt her hand and found it cold. "Esther, are you cold?"

"Yes." She looked at him. "Lately, I'm always cold."

Though Sam was warm, he started a fire and held a heavy blanket close to the flames to warm it before he wrapped it around her.

"Thank you, Sammy. That's much better." She was quiet for a minute. "Sam, if something were to happen to me, would you bury me in the meadow where we had the first picnic with the boys?"

Sam shuddered. "Esther honey, what are you talking about?"

"You never know when it might happen, Sammy. If I did pass on, I would like to be buried there."

"Alright," he said, wanting to get off the subject.

"Sam, do you remember when we first came to Montana? You said we'd grow old here together."

"Yes, I remember."

"I thought that was a wonderful thing to look forward to, and it is. Just think, though, in Heaven we'll be together for eternity, and we'll never grow old."

He hugged her and said, "What a blessed thought."

That night, Montana began running a fever. Though Esther herself was not well, she went to his side. All night long, she stayed close to him, bathing his forehead and praying for him. By morning, he was better.

Sam's heart was touched at the tenderness of his wife. She loved her family and put them first. Sam thought about how the Lord put the needs of man before His own. Esther was a wonderful example of Christ's true love.

Chapter 26

The Quarrel

Sam was worried about Esther. It seemed that her health failed more every day.

July was hot. Sam was working on a break in the fence when his hand slipped and the barbed wire cut into it. He winced and quickly wrapped his bandana around it to stop the bleeding.

"Hey, Sammy boy," Tom called cheerfully as he rode up.

Sam whirled around, his face red with anger. "Don't you ever call me that again! That was my father's name for me!"

"Sam, don't get mad," Tom said, sliding off his horse.

"Mad! What do you mean, don't get mad? Nothing is going right! My wife is sick! This wire's worthless! I don't know why I let you talk me into using barbed wire! I've never liked it!"

Tom was mad. "Now wait just a minute. It was your idea to fence in the land. Don't blame it all on me!"

"I'll tell you one thing," Sam said. "I'm about sick of this ranching together."

"Fine. If you want, we'll split up."

"Suits me!"

The two men mounted and rode off to their homes.

Tom stormed into the house and threw his hat to the ground. Carol came out of the kitchen.

"Tommy, what's wrong?" she asked in alarm.

"I'll tell you what's wrong. That Sam Goodton's got some nerve." He told Carol what had happened, and tears formed in Carol's eyes.

Tom marched to the bedroom. He was going to lie down, but Carol's Bible lay open on the bed. He was about to close it when he noticed that she had underlined a verse, Genesis 45:24. He read it. "So he sent his brethren away, and they departed: and he said unto them, See that ye fall not out by the way."

Tom wondered why Joseph gave that warning to his brothers. He read more. A famine had come and only Egypt had corn. Joseph's brothers had come to buy food and found that the brother they sold into slavery was a ruler in Egypt, second only to Pharaoh. Joseph had forgiven his brothers and was sending them home to take food to their families to keep them from starving.

What would cause these boys to fall out? Tom asked himself. As he thought about the brothers, he began to understand. They could have argued about their possessions, not wanting to give up the things God asked for. Pharaoh had told the sons of Jacob that if they came to Egypt he would give them what they needed but he told them to, "regard not your stuff;" In verse eighteen, he told them, "And take your father and your households, and come unto me: and I will give you the good of the land of Egypt, and ye shall eat the fat of the land." In verse twenty, he told them that "the good of all the land of Egypt is your's." Tom knew that there were times God said, "I want you to do this," but Christians let their possessions get in the way. They would not accept the fact that God had something better for them.

They might have argued about God's provision. Joseph gave Benjamin more gifts than the other brothers, and that could have caused them to get angry. Tom had seen people get upset because they felt that God did not do for them what He had done for others but the Bible plainly says that God is "no respecter of persons:" and whatever He gives is just right for that individual.

They also could have argued about their past—past sins and past problems with one another. They had sold their brother into slavery and lied to their father, but Joseph had forgiven them. Tom had met Christians who worried about their past, even though they were saved and their past sins were under the blood.

He closed the Bible and considered what he had learned. Joseph was a picture of God. The brothers represented Christians, and the family represented the lost world. The things those brothers could have fought over— possessions, God's provision, and past sins— were the same things that caused Christians to get crossways with each other.

He thought about how angry he was at Sam. Was it worth ruining their testimony and friendship? Was this little hurt worth "falling out" of the will of God? Tom knew it did not mean he would lose his salvation, for God is the Author of eternal salvation, but he knew he could lose his fellowship.

Tom knelt by the bed and begged the forgiveness of God. Then he went to apologize to Sam, first stopping at the kitchen where Carol was on her knees praying. Tom knelt beside her. "It's okay, Carol. I got it right."

Sam, meanwhile, had told Esther about the fight. Esther had never seen Sam so furious. *Lord, please help us*, she pleaded.

"Tom had no right to say what he said," Sam said angrily.

Esther was having one of her bad days. She struggled to her feet and walked slowly to her husband's side.

"Sam," she said, laying her hand on his arm. "I know it hurt you, but . . ." She really did not know what to say. "Sam, do you remember what we read in devotions this morning?"

"No, I don't," he admitted.

"We read Matthew five. Will you read it again, please?"

He sighed. "If you want me to." He grabbed his Bible and plopped onto the bed. He found Matthew 5 and began to read. He wished he had never consented to read the passage. It was the beatitudes.

"Blessed are the poor in spirit: for theirs is the kingdom of heaven.

"Blessed are they that mourn: for they shall be comforted.

"Blessed are the meek: for they shall inherit the earth.

"Blessed are they which do hunger and thirst after righteousness: for they shall be filled.

"Blessed are the merciful: for they shall obtain mercy.

"Blessed are the pure in heart: for they shall see God.

"Blessed are the peacemakers: for they shall be called the children of God.

"Blessed are they which are persecuted for righteousness' sake: for theirs is the kingdom of heaven.

"Blessed are ye, when men shall revile you, and persecute you, and shall say all manner of evil against you falsely, for my sake.

"Rejoice, and be exceeding glad: for great is your reward in heaven: for so persecuted they the prophets which were before you.

"Ye are the salt of the earth: but if the salt have lost his savour, wherewith shall it be salted? it is thenceforth good for nothing, but to be cast out, and to be trodden under foot of men."

As Sam read on, his conviction deepened.

"Ye have heard that it hath been said, Thou shalt love thy neighbour, and hate thine enemy.

"But I say unto you, Love your enemies, bless them that curse you, do good to them that hate you, and pray for them which despitefully use you, and persecute you;"

Love my enemies, Sam thought to himself. *Those that act hatefully toward me. Why*? The last verses answered his question.

"That ye may be the children of your Father which is in heaven: for he maketh his sun to rise on the evil and on the good, and sendeth rain on the just and on the unjust.

"For if ye love them which love you, what reward have ye? do not even the publicans the same?

"And if ye salute your brethren only, what do ye more than others? do not even the publicans so?

"Be ye therefore perfect, even as your Father which is in heaven is perfect."

Apparently there is a reward if you love them that don't love you, Sam thought. *What kind of rewards? Well, verse forty-five says others will see Jesus in you. Then, if you obey God then He can help straighten the situation out. The last verse says to be perfect, but I can't be perfect because I still have this old flesh that wants to do wrong.*

Sam realized that this perfection was not sinless perfection but perfect in that you grow up in your spiritual life.

"This whole mess is ridiculous, isn't it?" Sam asked.

Esther nodded. He chuckled dryly at her honesty. Then he knelt to pray.

"I'm sorry, Lord. Please forgive me. I forgive Tom for what he said. Please help me apologize to him. Help our friendship to be put back together and help me not to act so foolishly. Also, thank You, Lord, for my wife." He stood up and hugged Esther.

"I'm sorry, Esther honey. I'll go apologize to Tom." Before stepping out he turned to her and said, "Thanks."

It was not long until the men found one another. It was hard for two grown men to admit they were wrong, but the minute they saw each other they clasped hands.

Sam stepped back and said, "Tommy, I'm sorry. I was wrong."

"That's okay. I was wrong, too. Sorry, I got mad."

"It's forgiven." Sam searched for the right words. "You don't want to split up do you?"

Tom grinned. "You start talking like that and I'm liable to get mad again," he teased, slapping his friend on the back. "You're stuck with me."

Sam laughed. "This calls for a celebration. What say tonight, you come over for supper?"

"We'll be there," Tom promised.

That was all that was needed.

Tom and Carol moved into the spare room of the Silver Arrow so Carol could help Esther and the boys do the housework. To make their tasks as enjoyable as possible, Carol would often make an adventure out of cleaning. If they were dusting, they sometimes pretended the dust was gold and that they were mountain men looking for it. If they were hanging clothes out to dry, at times they pretended they were lost in some far off land and were making shelters to live in.

The boys also liked to sing and they would take turns singing their favorite hymns. Esther had been teaching them harmony, and they enjoyed experimenting, sometimes singing four parts. The younger boys, Montana and Martin, usually sang the melody while Matthew, Mike, and Mac filled in below.

Chapter 27

Until the Morning

The doctor had bad news. Esther was not well, and by the end of July she could barely get out of bed.

"Greg, isn't there anything we can do?" Sam asked when he and the doctor were alone.

The doctor shook his head. "I'm sorry, Sam." He laid his hand on the trembling man's shoulder. "I'm afraid she won't be with us much longer."

Sam turned away and wept. Dr. James stood silently, devastated and helpless. "I can see myself out," he said softly.

As soon as the doctor left, Tom came to Sam. He searched for words. Finally, he just put his arm around him and wept with his friend.

Carol came in. "Sam," she said in a broken voice, "Esther wants you."

Sam stood up and dried his eyes. He had to be strong for his wife. He took a moment to ask for God's help and went to her side.

He expected to see her lying on the bed in tears, but instead she was looking out the window with a smile on her face. When he came in, she turned to look at him.

"Sammy," she said as he sat down beside her. "My dear Sammy, I know it will probably happen." Her words were soft and loving.

Sam dropped his head. The tears were falling again, and he could not stop them. "Oh, Esther, Esther honey." He took her small hand in his.

"It's alright, Sam," she comforted. "It's not goodbye. It's simply goodnight. For when you say goodnight to someone, you expect to see them again in the morning, and there will be a glorious morning. Remember Romans 8:28? That's the verse I've claimed for my illness. Won't you claim it too? God will work everything out for good. He makes no mistakes."

Sam listened in wonder as she spoke. She was so free of fear. Death held no dread for Esther. She knew Heaven awaited her.

"I'll claim that verse," he promised.

"Sam, should we tell the boys?"

Pain as sharp as cold steel pierced his heart, causing Sam's tears to fall harder. His boys. What would they do without her? How could they live without her?

God, what are You doing? Sam cried inwardly.

"Sam?"

"I don't know. What do you think?"

"Call them in, one at a time, and I'll talk to them." Even before Sam left the room, Esther began to pray for wisdom.

Matthew came in first. He knew something was wrong and was trying to be brave.

Esther motioned him to come near. He sat as close to her as he could, and she put her arm around him.

"Mom, are you going to die?"

"Only God knows for certain, Warrior, but it looks like it's possible."

He began to weep. He buried his face in her shoulder and she held him close.

"Matthew, I want you to know that I'm saved. Are you?"

He could barely get the word *yes* out.

"Then if it does happen, we'll see each other again. I'll be in Heaven waiting for you.

Maybe you'll have a wife and children by then, and we'll meet up there."

"Mom," he said as he sat up. "How am I going to make it until then?"

She brushed away his tears. "God will give you grace if you trust in Him. He knows what is best. Never forget that. No matter what He does, it's right. Do you remember in the Bible when Jesus raised Lazarus from the dead?" When he nodded, she continued, "Remember, they said that if Jesus would have come right away, He could have healed Lazarus? Well, Jesus had a better plan. He was going to raise him from the dead, and God got greater glory. God knew what was best." She caressed his cheek. "Warrior, will you try to be strong for your brothers and your father? They'll need you. I'm not asking you to be perfect, but will you trust God and try to help the others trust Him, too? Your brothers look up to you. Don't forget that they are watching you. Remember what we learned in the Bible about being a leader, and put it to use." She paused and smiled lovingly at her son. "Will you try?"

He squared his shoulders and took a deep breath. "By God's grace, I'll try."

"Thank you, Matthew. I made a small pillow with a verse on it. It's my prayer for you."

The pillow was dark blue, and stitched on it with white thread were the words, "Above all, taking the shield of faith, wherewith ye shall be able to quench all the fiery darts of the wicked. Ephesians 6:16."

"Doubts and fears are going to come, but Warrior, you have a shield that can defeat those doubts. Remember, God makes no mistakes."

"Thanks. I love you, Mom."

"I love you, Matthew." She sent him downstairs to get Mike.

The older twin entered the room and smiled at Esther as he sat down beside her. She told him what might happen. He swallowed hard and began to cry.

Esther held him and told him she was saved and asked if he was. He said he was.

"So, I will see you in Heaven one day. Won't I, Mom?"

"You sure will, Professor, and until that day, trust that God will help you."

"I'm gonna miss you," he said tearfully.

"I'm sure that in Heaven I'll be wishing for you to come," she assured him. "Professor, do you remember what we learned about wisdom?"

"Yes, Mom."

"Who is wisest of all?"

"God."

"Can God make a mistake?"

"No."

"Then remember, God knows what He is doing, even when your wisdom can't figure it out. God knows best. I'm giving you a pillow with a verse on it. When you get confused, think about this verse."

The pillow was like Matthew's except that it was brown. The verse was Isaiah 40:14: "With whom took he counsel, and who instructed him, and taught him in the path of judgment, and taught him knowledge, and shewed to him the way of understanding?"

He hugged the pillow tightly. "God knows best," he repeated.

"I love you, Mike."

"I love you, Mom."

MacShane came in next. Such a big boy he was, yet tender in personality.

As with the other two, she explained the danger. Holding him close as he wept, she reached for his pillow.

"This is for you, Lumberjack. I made it. The verse on it is to help you. You're going to face things that you can't lick in your own strength, things like death, fear, questions, sickness. But there is a God Who can help you. Are you saved, MacShane?"

He nodded.

"So am I. So one day we'll be together again in Heaven. We'll walk hand in hand on golden streets. We'll see Jesus and praise Him forever."

"I can't wait."

"Me neither, but until then, remember this verse: Ephesians 6:10, 'Finally, my brethren, be strong in the Lord, and in the power of his might.' Trust in Him, for He makes no mistakes."

He stroked the soft black material. "Mom, I'll always keep this pillow on my bed," he promised. "I love you."

"I love you."

Montana came in. He was in such contrast to Mac. Though he was almost as tall, he weighed about half as much. The bed hardly creaked as he cuddled near his mother. She told him what was going on and asked him if he was saved. He said yes. She spoke of

Heaven and the fact that they would be together there.

"Once we get to Heaven, we'll never be separated again."

"Never?" he asked, wiping away his tears.

"Never, but until that time, hardships will come, Soldier. God has a reason for everything He does, though. Do you remember when Uncle Shane told us about the time his captain ordered him to do something that he didn't understand, but he did it anyway?"

"Yes, and they won the battle!"

She laughed. "Yes. The Captain knew something that Uncle Shane didn't know. God is our Captain. He knows so much more than we do, and He never makes a mistake. So when He asks you to do something that you don't understand, remember this verse: II Timothy 2:3, 'Thou therefore endure hardness, as a good soldier of Jesus Christ.'"

She handed the dark red pillow to the boy. Again he read the verse stitched in white with such love, care, and prayer.

"I love you, Montana."

"I love you, Mommy."

Esther waited nervously for her youngest son. How could she comfort Martin? The boy was not saved, and he had no hope of Heaven. How could she show him his need of a Saviour?

"Lord, please help me," she prayed.

The door opened and Martin bounded in, such a carefree boy. When Esther motioned him to come to her, he ran to the bed, jumped on, did a summersault, and landed by her side.

"Tornado," she said slowly, "I need to tell you something."

"What?"

"Do you know what it means to die?"

Martin's face turned white.

"You know Momma's been sick, and she's not getting better. So, it looks like Momma may die."

"No!" he screamed. "No! No! No!" He kept screaming and began to flail his arms.

Those in the living room could hear him. Sam almost rushed to the room but decided that Esther needed to be alone with Martin. Instead, he pulled Montana close.

Matthew was sitting with Aunt Carol. She had her arm around him. The twins were with

Uncle Tom. All four of the boys, held their pillows close.

Finally, Esther was able to get hold of her son and pull him close to her. He threw his arms around her neck and cried. She comforted him.

"My baby," she soothed. "My precious baby boy. Listen to me, Martin. Your mother is saved and she's going to Heaven. There nothing will ever hurt her again. Her health will be perfect. She'll be with Jesus, and He will take good care of her."

"We can take care of you," he whispered.

"Oh, I know that, son, but it looks like God wants me to be with Him soon. I don't know why, but I trust God that He makes no mistakes."

"Mom, I'm not going to Heaven."

"Do you know why?"

He nodded and sat back. "Jesus said that you have to get saved to go to Heaven. I've never been saved."

"Why not, Marty?"

"Because I didn't want to be. I didn't want to admit that I was bad enough to go to hell, but I know I am. I want to get saved."

"Martin, the Bible asks, 'Can two walk together, except they be agreed?' You can't walk with God if you won't agree with Him. Repentance is agreeing with God."

"I know." He bowed his head and began to pray, "Dear Jesus, I'm sorry. You said that all have sinned and that means me. I wouldn't listen to what Momma and Daddy and Pastor told me about getting saved, and I'm sorry. I know You're the only One that can get me to Heaven. Please save me. Amen."

Esther could barely refrain from weeping. God had answered their prayers. Not only had all five of her sons gotten saved, but she had lived to see it. *Thank You, my Lord. O thank You, Jesus*, she prayed.

"Martin, I have something for you."

"Is it a pillow?" Esther nodded. "I saw that the other boys had one. What are they?"

"I made you each a pillow with a special Bible verse on it. As time passes and hardships come, remember this verse: Proverbs 3:5, 'Trust in the LORD with all thine heart; and lean not unto thine own understanding.' Trust God, Martin. Trust Him to guide you, for He makes no mistakes. Now, go tell the others that you got saved."

"I love you, Mommy."

"I love you, Martin."

The boy jumped off the bed and raced down to the living room.

Esther lay on the bed. The emotional talks had drained what little strength she had, but there was a peace in her heart. There was fear, too. Fear of what would happen to her family after she left.

"God, I am afraid for my husband and boys. Afraid that perhaps they will become angry and stop serving You. If it is Thy will that I go, please help them. Help Sam to keep serving You. Help Matthew to be filled with wisdom in leading his brothers. Help Mike to be wise in spiritual things. Help Mac to be strong in the Lord. I pray Montana will be a good soldier for You. And Martin, thank You that he trusted Christ as his Saviour. Lord, he is so lighthearted. I fear that he'll make spur of the moment decisions that he will regret. I pray he'll follow You."

When she came in the next morning with Esther's breakfast, it was obvious that Carol had spent the night in tears.

"Hi," was the cheeriest greeting she could muster.

"Hi," Esther replied. "Carol, would you open the chest at the foot of the bed? There's a box in it to the right. Would you bring it to me, please?"

"Of course." Carol set down her tray of food and opened the chest. When she found the box, she took it to Esther.

Esther lifted the lid and pulled out the baby blanket she had made. "For your baby, Carol, and I made a pillow for it, too. I want you to give these to your baby for me."

"Maybe you can do it, when the time comes," Carol said hopefully.

"Maybe, but just in case, take these, please."

With trembling hands, Carol accepted the gifts. The pillow was white with dark blue letters. The verse was Psalms 145:9, "The LORD is good to all: and his tender mercies are over all his works."

"It's beautiful, Esther. Thank you."

"You're welcome. Now tell me, what names have you picked out for the baby?"

Carol gave a weak laugh. "Tom doesn't want to pick out names. He says he wants to see it first before we decide on a name. That's fine with me."

"What does Tom want, boy or girl?"

Carol sat down on a chair beside Esther. "I think he would like a girl. He's used to talk about giving his mom and dad a granddaughter, since they never had a daughter. He doesn't really care, though. We're both just so happy we're going to have a baby. But if Tom could decide, he would have a girl, I think. I would, too."

"I hope it's a girl," Esther said, her expression warm and serene.

"Tom's made toys by the dozens for the baby, and he's working on a beautiful crib. It would look right at home in some king's nursery." Carol smiled. "Tom's not the only one making things. I've made outfits for both boys and girls. Whichever ones I don't need, I'll give away. The baby will have enough clothes to last it for about a year." She sighed happily. "I can't wait."

August 2 was a Wednesday. Despite her illness, Esther wanted to go to church. The next day they had the birthday party for the boys. Matthew turned ten, the twins were nine, Montana was eight, and Martin was seven. They also celebrated being in Montana for three years.

The following Monday, Esther knew her time was nearly over.

"Sam," she whispered. He was sitting close to her side. "Call the boys."

"Esther, no. Please Esther, I can't live without you. I need you."

"Remember our verse? 'And we know that all things work together for good to them that love God, to them who are the called according to his purpose.'"

"But, Esther, not this," he pleaded.

She took hold of his hand. "Please, Sam, call the boys."

Sam ran from the room and out the door. "Clint!" he yelled. The ranch hand jumped the corral and came running.

"Get the doctor! Hurry!" Sam begged. Clint grabbed the nearest horse and raced off to town.

Tom and Carol were in the garden. They heard Sam's cries and came running. Together, they rushed to Esther's side.

"Carol, stay with her. I have to get the boys," Sam said. He quickly rounded up his sons and brought them to the room.

"Esther," he said, "Clint went to get the doctor. Hang on, Esther honey. Hang on."

Duke whined and put his front paws on the bed.

"Gather close," she whispered.

When they did, they saw her lips moving but could not hear her. Matthew, trembling with unbelief, remembered that his mother asked him to be strong. He looked around. The others were so numbed by what was happening that they were not trying to listen.

Help me, Lord, Matthew prayed. He drew as close to her as he could. "Mom," he said softly, "we can't hear you. Can you talk a little louder?"

Sam would remember the next moment as a parting gift from God, because Esther suddenly gained strength. Her words were clear, and she was singing.

"At the cross, at the cross,
Where I first saw the light.
And the burden of my heart rolled way.
It was there by faith,
I received my sight.
And now I am happy all the day."

She raised her hand and waved weakly. "Good night, my beloved ones."

Chapter 28

Not My Will

Sam had never felt so utterly bewildered. Tom and Carol sent telegrams to the family and made all the arrangements for the funeral. It was held the next day in the meadow that Esther loved.

The casket lay on the ground with a few late blooming bitterroots around it. Esther was beautiful. She was wrapped in the shawl that Sam had bought in Minneapolis. Ralf and Clint had dug the grave and had gathered two wheelbarrows full of sparkling stones to spread over it after the ceremony. Brother Holte fashioned a lovely cross to place at the head.

Pastor McBride stood before the group of people.

"Folks, we are gathered here to say 'good night' to a loved one." He paused and wiped tears from his eyes. "We say good night because we expect the morning to come. We expect the Lord to one day call His children home to Heaven. What makes Heaven so

sweet? I believe the answer is found in
Revelation chapter five, beginning in verse six.

> "And I beheld, and, lo, in the midst of
> the throne and of the four beasts, and in
> the midst of the elders, stood a Lamb as
> it had been slain, having seven horns
> and seven eyes, which are the seven
> Spirits of God sent forth into all the earth.
> "And he came and took the book out of
> the right hand of him that sat upon the
> throne.
> "And when he had taken the book, the
> four beasts and four and twenty elders
> fell down before the Lamb, having every
> one of them harps, and golden vials full
> of odours, which are the prayers of
> saints.
> "And they sung a new song, saying,
> Thou art worthy to take the book, and to
> open the seals thereof: for thou wast
> slain, and hast redeemed us to God by
> thy blood out of every kindred, and
> tongue, and people, and nation;
> "And hast made us unto our God kings
> and priests: and we shall reign on the
> earth.

"And I beheld, and I heard the voice of many angels round about the throne and the beasts and the elders: and the number of them was ten thousand times ten thousand, and thousands of thousands;

"Saying with a loud voice, Worthy is the Lamb that was slain to receive power, and riches, and wisdom, and strength, and honour, and glory, and blessing.

"And every creature which is in heaven, and on the earth, and under the earth, and such as are in the sea, and all that are in them, heard I saying, Blessing, and honour, and glory, and power, be unto him that sitteth upon the throne, and unto the Lamb for ever and ever.

"And the four beasts said, Amen. And the four and twenty elders fell down and worshipped him that liveth for ever and ever."

"I read in this passage about Heaven. Heaven is our home. What is so special about home? If we could use only one word to describe home, it would have to be the word *familiar*. Home is a place filled with familiar people, things, smells, and sounds. As I read about Heaven, I find that it is filled with familiar things.

"First of all, I am familiar with the Prince of that city. I know God. We read here about a Lamb slain before the foundation of the world. Do you know Who that Lamb is? It's Jesus. Jesus is in Heaven, and I'm familiar with Him. No, I've never seen Him with these eyes, I've never heard His voice with these ears, and I've never touched Him with these hands. By faith, I saw Him on Calvary, dying for me. By faith, I heard Him say, 'Come unto me, all ye that labour and are heavy laden, and I will give you rest. Take my yoke upon you, and learn of me; for I am meek and lowly in heart: and ye shall find rest unto your souls. For my yoke is easy, and my burden is light.' By faith, I trusted Him as my Saviour. These past years, I've tried to learn more about Him. I've learned about His love, His life, and His leadership, and when I get to Heaven it won't be strange to me to hear Him and see Him.

"Secondly, I'm familiar with the practices of that city. Do you know what we're going to do in Heaven? The last verses of our passage tell us. We will be praising the Lord. We'll be saying—" He stopped and looked over the crowd. "We'll be saying to the Lord, 'You did it just right. I didn't understand it, but You did it just right.'"

Matthew and his brothers exchanged glances. They remembered their mother saying, "God makes no mistakes."

This sure looks like a mistake, God, Matthew thought. *I don't understand.* He remembered his mother's verse in Romans: "And we know that all things work together for good..." Did God really have good planned? He turned his attention back to the message.

"And there is one more thing," Pastor McBride said. "I'm familiar with the population of that city. I know some of the people up there. I've never met the prophets of old, but I've studied them and I know about them. So when I get to Heaven and Jonah starts to talk about when he was swallowed by the great fish, I'll be familiar with that. I know some preachers up there—men like Jake Griggs, Jack Johnson, and William Kell—my mentors, who taught me much about God and His Word.

"I also know some precious people up there."

People in the crowd began to weep as they thought of loved ones. Sam, Tom, and Carol cuddled the five boys close as they wept.

"Many of you have family and friends in Heaven," he said compassionately. "I do, too. My parents are in Heaven, and I have a sister there. Now, our sister in the Lord, Esther Goodton, is in Heaven. Mrs. Goodton was a wonderful person. She was caring and loving and faithful, but that's not why she is in Heaven. Good works can't get you there. Jesus told Nicodemus in John 3:3, 'Verily, verily, I say unto thee, Except a man be born again, he cannot see the kingdom of God.'

"How does one be born again? When the Philippian jailor asked Paul and Silas how to be saved, they said, 'Believe on the Lord Jesus Christ, and thou shalt be saved, and thy house.'

"We know by her own testimony, which many of you have heard, that Esther was saved. She accepted Christ as her Saviour. She didn't trust in the fact that her parents were Christians. She didn't trust in her good works. She didn't trust in baptism or church membership. She trusted in Christ Jesus. She put her faith in what Jesus did on Calvary.

"Paul said in Acts 20:21 that he had testified 'both to the Jews, and also to the Greeks, repentance toward God, and faith toward our Lord Jesus Christ.' What is repentance? He tells us in Acts 19:4 that John the Baptist 'baptized with the baptism of repentance, saying unto the people, that they should believe on him which should come after him, that is, on Christ Jesus.'

"Folks, we can all see Mrs. Esther again. If you too will trust Christ as your Saviour, you will be in that number when the saints of God, those who are saved, are called up to Heaven."

Pastor McBride prayed and closed his Bible. Carol removed the shawl from Esther's body and handed it to Sam. The ranch hands picked up the casket and began to lower it into the ground as the McBrides sang "At the Cross."

Tom was trying to comfort Carol and the twins while Sam held the two younger boys. Matthew had stepped back to let his brothers be with the adults. He was trying to be strong for them as his mother had asked, but his heart was breaking. Just when he felt his strength was gone, a pair of arms engulfed him.

"Uncle Shane," he cried.

"It's okay, Matthew," Shane said through his tears. "Your momma wouldn't mind if you cried, and neither does God. Go ahead and cry, son."

With the grave covered and the rocks in place, Sam turned to head for the wagon. It was not until then that he saw Shane. Matthew was still in his arms.

"Shane? Shane, when did you get here?" He seemed to be in a daze.

Shane could barely control his tears. "I . . . I . . . was coming . . . to . . . to visit. What . . . happened?"

Sam could not tell him. His heart would not allow it. Tom explained.

Shane looked at the grave and felt that he was going to be sick. Esther was no longer with them. How could it be?

Duke lay on the grave, whining softly. Sam did not call him. He let him stay with the woman he adored.

The Goodtons, Sampsons, and Shane went to the Meadowlark. The Silver Arrow held too many memories.

That night, the two families skipped supper for no one was hungry. Matthew left the family in the living room and stepped out on the porch. He wanted to be alone.

A few minutes later, the door opened. Uncle Tom came and sat beside him. After several moments, Tom spoke.

"Look at all the stars."

Matthew looked up at the millions of stars.

"Matty, did you know God has every one of the stars named?"

The question startled Matthew. He knew they were named, but he had never given the idea much thought.

"Wow," he said.

"That's right. Psalms 147:4 says, 'He telleth the number of the stars; he calleth them all by their names.'"

They were quiet again until a bird began to sing.

"Did you know that He takes care of all the birds? 'Behold the fowls of the air: for they sow not, neither do they reap, nor gather into barns; yet your heavenly Father feedeth them.' He even cares for the little sparrow. 'Are not five sparrows sold for two farthings, and not one of them is forgotten before God?'"

Matthew had read the verses, but that night the realization that God took care of every bird stirred him.

"That's a big God," Matthew said.

"Yes, He is." Tom put his arm around the boy. "He's big enough to keep track of the stars and the birds, and big enough to know what you're going through. I know this is hard, and God knows that. He loves you, Matthew. He knows exactly how you feel, and He will help you." He hugged Matthew and went back inside.

Matthew looked up at the night sky and whispered, "God makes no mistakes." That night Matthew began a habit of looking at the stars whenever his trials were too big to understand, and always he was reminded of the bigness of God.

By the end of the week, the elder Goodtons, the Makers, and Ty and C were there.

The moment Tyler walked in the door, Sam rushed to him. Tyler was taken aback. Sam had been the strong one of the two. Tyler had leaned on his shoulder, but it was Sam who needed to lean on someone this time. *Help,*

Lord, Tyler prayed as he held tightly to his older brother.

Sam took the Makers to the graveside. Laramie and Lisa looked down at the ground that covered their daughter.

"I'm so sorry," Sam said, feeling responsible for her death.

Lisa turned and hugged her son-in-law. "No, Sam. It's not your fault. Esther was happy. I can't tell you how many times she wrote us and said how much she loved it here. I'm glad she got to experience this place. Don't blame yourself. God knew Esther would go, and to know she left with peace, surrounded by those she loved, and in a home she loved somehow helps ease the pain."

Mr. Maker nodded and laid his hand on Sam's shoulder.

Having his parents with him helped Sam immensely. Just knowing they were there was an encouragement. The boys were glad to have their family with them, but soon the family had to make plans to leave. There were things at home in Indiana that could not be left unattended.

"Tom."

Tom was cleaning out a stall when Sam and Duke entered the barn.

"Yeah, Sam."

"Tom, I'm leaving," Sam said.

Tom sighed. "Are you sure?"

"I can't live here. Not without her," Sam said. "I can't."

"Okay, but will you pray and make sure. If its God's will, I understand."

"I will pray."

Sam went to his home and stepped into his room. Everything there reminded him of Esther. He fell on the bed weeping.

"Oh God, why?" he whispered. "Why my Esther? Lord, I know You make no mistakes, and I'm not angry with You, but why? How can all this work? What do I do? Do I stay here? I don't know if I can. Do I leave? That's what I want to do. I want to go far away from this place. What do I do?"

Will I obey Him if He tells me to do what I don't want to do? The question was profound. He remembered Jesus' prayer, when He was getting ready to go to the cross: "Father, if thou be willing, remove this cup from me: nevertheless not my will, but thine, be done." Jesus was willing to do whatever His Father wanted. Sam wanted to go back to Indiana, but what did God want? A mighty struggle was going on inside Samuel Goodton.

Finally, he sank to his knees. "Dear God..." The words could not get past the tears. He finally said, "Not . . . my will . . . but . . . Thine."

Sam was crying so hard that he needed a handkerchief. Forgetting he was on Esther's side of the bed, he reached into her dresser drawer. He drew out several sheets of paper.

"What's this?" he asked aloud. He looked at the first one and caught his breath. The date was around the time that Esther got sick. As Sam read, he realized that she had left a diary of prayers she had prayed during her illness.

Sam sat down and thumbed through them. He stopped at the next to the last one.

"Dear God, I think I am dying. I won't mention it yet in case I'm wrong, but I think I will not live to see my boys grown. Lord, if it is Thy will that I go, I pray that You will help my family. I pray for Sam, Matthew, Mike, MacShane, Monty, and Marty. I pray they will stay in Montana. I don't know why, but I think that You have great plans

*for them here. But if You want them to go
back to Indiana, Thy will be done."*

Sam folded the papers and his tears began
to fall afresh. "Okay, Lord. I'll stay. I don't
know how, but we'll stay. Please help us."

The boys were glad they were going to stay
in Montana. They loved the ranch as much as
Esther did. The Makers and Goodtons were
glad, too. Though they would have loved to
have Sam and the boys close, they believed
that God had plans for them where they were.

So it was with mixed emotions that
goodbyes were said that Monday, two weeks
after Esther's homegoing.

Chapter 29

God Makes No Mistakes

Sam could not believe the weather. It was January 6, yet most of the snow was gone and the sun was shining. He was glad because he could be outside and keep his mind busy with work. He tried his best to include his sons in everything he did.

"Sam, I'm taking Carol to the doctor."

"Is everything alright?" Sam asked anxiously.

"Yes," Tom quickly assured him. "We want to be near the doctor when the time comes. Remember, we talked about staying with the Kenneths?"

"I remember now." He chuckled dryly. "I seem to forget things easy."

"You look tired, Sam."

"I am tired, but when I close my eyes I see . . . I see . . . her," he finished, unable to say her name.

Tom stepped closer and laid his hand on Sam's shoulder. "Lord, we know that You are in control. Still, sometimes we get to worrying about things and it keeps us awake. Please, help Sammy. I pray, that at night, he and the boys would be able to sleep. We thank You for what You are going to do. Amen."

"Thanks, Tommy. I'm glad that we settled our argument."

"Me, too." Turning to leave, he stopped and faced Sam. "Sam, I love you like a brother. You know that right?"

"I do know that, and I love you, too." They embraced and Sam followed him to the buggy.

"Carol, you take care," Sam said. "I can't wait to see the baby."

"Me, too," Tom said, jumping in next to his wife.

"Me, three," she said excitedly.

"So long," they called as the wagon pulled out.

"So long," Sam answered with a wave of his hand.

Around 9:00 that night, Duke stood up and barked softly. Sam recognized the bark. Someone the dog knew was coming. In a moment, there was a knock on the door of the Silver Arrow.

Who could that be? Sam wondered. The boys were in bed and Sam was getting ready to go himself. There was a second knock. Sam made sure his pistol was loaded.

"Who is it?" he called.

"Its me, Sam, Sheriff Elwood."

Recognizing the voice, Sam laid aside his pistol and opened the door. "Well, Sheriff, what brings—" The look on Keith Elwood's face gave Sam chills. Randall Holte and Pastor McBride were there, too. Something was wrong.

"What is it, Keith?"

"Sam, are the boys in bed?" Sam nodded, too afraid for words. "Will you come out on the porch?"

Sam stepped outside and shut the door.

"Sam," the sheriff began slowly, "I—I don't know how to tell you this, but Tom and Carol had an accident."

Sam's heart fell.

"They were coming across that rough stretch of ground you folks call Rocky-land. A rabbit spooked the horses. They took off and Tom couldn't hold them. The wagon hit a patch of ice, tipped, and they were both thrown."

Sam tried to talk but could only shake his head.

"Randall and Barb saw it," Pastor McBride said emotionally. "They tried to help them but..." The pastor paused, not knowing how to finish the sentence.

"No!" Sam cried. "Dear God, please no. Not Esther, Tom, Carol, and the baby. Oh, no!" He fell to his knees and wept. The three men knelt beside him.

"Sam," the pastor said gently, putting his arm around him. "The baby didn't die."

Sam was weeping so hard that at first he did not hear him.

"Sam, the baby did not die," Brother McBride had to repeat himself four times before Sam heard.

"What?" Sam asked as the full impact of what was being said struck him.

"Carol lived long enough to have the baby," Mr. Holte explained. "They both got to hold her for a few minutes. I've...I've...never seen anything like it. Barb delivered the baby. She wrapped her in a blanket and laid her in Carol's arms. Carol kissed the baby's cheek and whispered, 'Thank You, Lord,' and she was gone. When we placed the baby in Tom's arms, he wept and said, 'God is good.' He kissed her and then he was gone."

Sam's tears of anguish became mingled with tears of joy. "So they both got to hold *her*? It was a girl?"

Randall nodded. "It's a girl, and she's healthy as can be. She's at the hospital in town. The nurses are caring for her."

Sam was flooded with conflicting emotions. Sorrow, because his best friends were gone. Joy, because they were able to hold the baby they loved so much. Peace, because God makes no mistakes. Hope, because a part of Tom and Carol was alive in that precious baby.

Suddenly, he remembered a promise made long ago. His mind went back to the day when he and Tom were young grooms-to-be. They were in Indiana, each helping the other build a house for himself and his bride-to-be. He could remember clearly that he was on the porch finishing the railing. Tom was on the ground building the steps. Tom had mentioned what a great privilege and responsibility he would be granted as head of his household. Then he had said, "I don't know why the Lord put this on my heart, Sammy, but He did, so I'll tell you. If you are ever hurt, I promise to help take care of your family. No matter where you are, if you need me, don't hesitate to send for me."

Sam had answered, "Same here. The Lord put it on my heart last night, too. I was going to tell you today, but you beat me to it. Only the Lord went a little deeper with me. If you were to . . . to . . ."

He remembered that he could not finish the sentence. Tom had said the word *die* and Sam had said that he would take care of his wife and children.

God had told Sam to make that promise, but did He want Sam to adopt Tom's baby girl?

"I can't, Lord," he whispered. "I don't know how to care for a girl. I just can't. Surely You don't want *me* to adopt her." Still, he remembered how the need to make that promise had burned within him.

"Do you want me to stay with you?" The question from Pastor McBride brought Sam back to the present.

"No, no, that'll be alright. Clint and Ralf will...they'll be here."

"Okay, Sam."

Sam paced the floor all night. He heard Clint and Raff talking quietly in the living room downstairs. He could tell they were praying. The news was hard on them, too. Ralf and Clint had become members of the family.

"God, what do I do?" he asked. Then he remembered the words, "Not my will but Thine."

"Lord, I'll do what You want, by Your grace." He opened his Bible. His devotion for the next day began in I Samuel 20.

> "And Jonathan said unto David, Come, and let us go out into the field. And they went out both of them into the field.
> "And Jonathan said unto David, O LORD God of Israel, when I have sounded my father about to morrow any time, or the third day, and, behold, if there be good toward David, and I then send not unto thee, and shew it thee;
> "The LORD do so and much more to Jonathan: but if it please my father to do thee evil, then I will shew it thee, and send thee away, that thou mayest go in peace: and the LORD be with thee, as he hath been with my father.

"And thou shalt not only while yet I live shew me the kindness of the LORD, that I die not:

"But also thou shalt not cut off thy kindness from my house for ever: no, not when the LORD hath cut off the enemies of David every one from the face of the earth.

"So Jonathan made a covenant with the house of David, saying, Let the LORD even require it at the hand of David's enemies."

Sam stopped reading and began to think about the verses. David and Jonathan were setting up a plan to see if Saul had determined evil against David. Jonathan and David were close friends, and Jonathan made David promise to show himself and his household kindness, even after Jonathan's death. He knew that David was God's anointed king, and he knew that one day David would sit on the throne.

Sam noticed a Bible reference that he had at one time written in the margin of his Bible. He quickly turned to 2 Samuel 9:1 and read, "And David said, Is there yet any that is left of the house of Saul, that I may shew him kindness for Jonathan's sake?"

David was on the throne. Jonathan had died, but David did not forget that promise. He "adopted" Jonathan's son Mephibosheth, a cripple and by birth an enemy of David. Still, David showed him kindness for Jonathan's sake. Sam remembered Pastor McBride preaching on the passage several months ago. He had explained that Mephibosheth was a picture of the sinner, that by birth every person is an enemy of God. Man was crippled by the fall of Adam and had no sure means of survival. Humanly speaking, God should have nothing to do with mankind, but because of the covenant between God the Father and God the Son, He shows mercy to anyone who will call upon Him.

"Thank You, Lord," Sam prayed, "for showing mercy to me and saving me, even though I didn't and still don't deserve it."

Sam thought of Tom's baby. What if for some reason her family back in Indiana could not take care of her? That baby would need someone. She would have no one to care for her, no one to bring her up in the admonition of the Lord. She would need Sam and his boys.

"Lord, I don't know how, but we'll try. If her family can't take her, we'll try."

The next morning Clint and Ralf arranged the funeral and sent telegrams. Sam had to tell his boys. For a good hour, he and his sons cried together. Then he told them about the baby, but he did not mention adopting her. First, he needed to let the Greys have a chance to adopt their granddaughter. The elder Sampsons could not care for her because of Joel's illness. Sam had to wait on God.

Chapter 30

The Master's Plan

They buried Tom and Carol next to Esther. Sam felt as if his world was caving in, yet a still, small voice in his heart kept whispering, "And we know that all things work together for good to them that love God..."

As soon as possible, Sam and his boys went to see the baby. She was beautiful—her hair golden, the color of a dandelion, and her eyes the deepest blue.

"It looks like she got all of Tom's blonde hair and all of Carol's golden hair. The same with her blue eyes," Sam said in wonder.

Matthew and his brothers crowded close to the crib.

"She's so small," Mike said.

For three weeks, Sam waited for word from Tom's and Carol's family. None came.

"Sam, we've got a problem."

Sam was at the doctor's office visiting the baby.

"What is it?"

"This town has a law that when a baby is not spoken for within four weeks, it is put up for adoption," the doctor explained.

"What? I haven't got word from her family yet."

Greg nodded. "I know, but that's the law here, and," he added, "the Donavans want her."

"The Donavans! Whatever for? They hardly knew Tom." Sam thought about the Donavans, a wealthy family with one young boy and a baby on the way. They were arrogant and rude. To them everyone else was a step lower. Sam and Tom and their wives had tried to befriend the new couple, but the Donavans wanted nothing to do with them. Sam had asked the Lord to help him change his feelings toward them and had tried to treat them right. The Lord had helped him learn to love and pray for them, but the thought of them having Tom's girl was frightening. The Donavans were not Christians. "They aren't godly people and would not raise her like Tom and Carol would have wanted."

"I know that, and I don't know why they want her," Greg admitted. "I *do* know that you're going to have a hard time keeping them from getting her. Just imagine what a court would think?"

"Court?" Sam exclaimed. "You mean I may have to go to court over her?"

"It could come to that. Sam, think about what a judge would think. He wouldn't know that you and Tom were best friends. He wouldn't know about your religious beliefs. On one hand, he would see a widower with five boys raising cattle on a ranch, and on the other would be the Donavans. They look like the better choice." Greg sighed. "You need a lawyer."

There was a knock on the door.

"Come in," Greg called.

A man walked in. Sam had seen him before but did not know him.

"Oh, hello Mr. PaDave. Ready for your appointment?" Greg asked.

"Yes and no. I heard your conversation," he said. He turned to Sam. "My name is Maxwell PaDave. I'm a lawyer, and I'll help you get that baby."

Sam was stunned and Greg grinned. "Now why didn't I think of you?"

The man smiled. "I have a godly family, and I want this baby you're talking about to have that blessing."

After talking to Maxwell, Sam was encouraged. The lawyer said that by law the child would go to her next of kin.

"Good," Sam said. "That means one of the Greys will get her." Just when he thought maybe things would work, he got a letter from the Greys.

"Dear Sam. God must have a reason. Oh, how we want to come out there, but the government is fighting. We finally got permission to accept black and Indian children at the orphanage, but some people in the town didn't like that. Someone lied to the authorities and told them that we were using the government's money to fill our own pockets and were neglecting the children. They're trying to shut us down. The government has told us we can't adopt any more children until this matter is settled, not even our granddaughter. In fact, we're not allowed to leave town. We know the government's not being cruel. They've been lied to and are trying to find the truth, but none of us can take our

granddaughter. Neither can Tiffany and Leah. Todd and Tessa are in Europe. There is no way to contact them in time to come and help you. Melissa and Jane are somewhere in Mexico. It would take a month to reach them, a month for them to get to a train station, and another several weeks to get to you. If we could reach them, we're told that because they are Indian they will not be able to adopt the baby. Joel and Virginia cannot take care of her. There is no way they could adopt her. This letter is so late in coming because we were searching every angle. You are our only hope. We pray for you."

Sam folded the letter and began to weep. "Lord, help us please. Thy will be done. I pray that Tom's girl will go to a Christian home if she can't go with us." It occurred to him that he still had not told his boys about adopting the baby. He decided it was time he did.

He called the boys to the living room.

"Time we talk heap much," he said, pretending he was an Indian chief. The boys laughed, and they all sat down Indian style.

Sam was not sure how to approach the subject, but he prayed for strength and tried to follow God's leadership. "Boys, Uncle Tom and Aunt Carol's baby is all alone. She has no one to care for her."

"What will happen to her?" Mac asked.

"Well, if no one adopts her, she could go to an orphanage."

"What's that?" Montana asked.

"It's a place where they put children who have no parents."

"The Greys have one don't they?" Mike asked.

"Yes."

"Are they nice?" Montana wanted to know.

"The Greys' is nice, but some aren't. Some don't teach about Jesus."

"How will she get saved?" Martin inquired.

"I don't know."

"Do all children that go to orphanages get adopted?" Matthew asked.

"No, and sometimes they get adopted into bad families. I got a letter from Uncle Tom and Aunt Carol's family. They can't adopt her. So . . ." He did not know how to finish.

"Then why don't we adopt her?" all five asked at once.

Sam's heart leaped for joy. *God makes no mistakes*, he thought to himself.

Sam took the Greys' letter to the lawyer. Max read it and shook his head. "This is bad."

"What can we do?" Sam asked.

"Well, since the normal legal action of turning custody over to the next of kin is impossible, she now becomes a true orphan. In a case where two families are attempting to adopt the child, it will have to be brought before a judge. Since Miles City does not have a permanent judge of its own yet, one will be sent from Helena. The judge presiding now is very sick so I don't know who will come in his place. He'll decide to whom the child will go. It depends on how he views the candidates."

"What would help us?" Sam asked.

The lawyer thought a moment. "Maybe—mind you, I said maybe—if you hired someone to care for the baby. An elderly couple that has raised children would be great. The judge might be more lenient to our side under those circumstances."

"Who should I consider?" Sam asked.

"I don't know. I haven't been in Miles City very long. Who do you know that would be good?"

Sam could not think of one couple. He knew there had to be someone, but none came to mind. The recent emotional shocks and hard work had muddled his thinking. Sometimes nothing seemed real.

Max saw how tired he was. "Sam," he said, laying his hand on his shoulder. "Go take a walk. Rest your mind. We can talk about this later. Besides getting a couple to help you, there's nothing we can do until the judge gets here except pray."

Sam nodded and left the office. As he shut the door, he heard Mr. PaDave praying.

He had been walking for several minutes when someone called his name. He turned to see an elderly man hastening toward him. Something about his energetic walk and cheery voice was vaguely familiar. A woman beside him walked with a slight limp. Who were they? Then the woman smiled at him, and things fell into place. They were Donnie and Tricia Pitt from his home church in Indiana. Sam hurried to greet them.

"Sam, it's good to see you," Donnie said, shaking his hand.

"I thought that you folks were in Delaware taking care of your daughter," Sam said.

"We were, but she's doing much better now. We thought about staying there, but after praying, we decided to move here. We know the McBrides and decided to join their church to see if we could be of help. In fact, we just arrived in town this week. Say, how are your family and Tom and Carol?"

Sam could no longer rein in his emotions. There on the street he poured his heart out to Donnie and Tricia Pitt.

"So," he finished, "if I can't find someone to help me, I may lose the baby, too."

"You've found someone," Donnie said.

"What?" Sam asked.

"Sam," Tricia began, "God told us to leave Delaware and come to Miles City. We thought it was to help the McBrides but now God has shown us why."

Sam was still confused.

"Sam," Donnie said, "we'll help you, if you want us to. We'll stay as long as needed."

Sam's sorrow turned to joy. While he had been complaining, God had already worked everything out.

"All things work together for good," was all that he could say.

Sam's lawyer was elated. Things were looking better.

That night before he went to bed, Sam read his Bible. God had helped him establish the habit when he was a little boy. He was reading in Ruth about a man named Elimelech. Elimelech left Bethlehem, the house of bread, because there was a famine in the land, and took his family to Moab, a place whose name meant "which father?" or "who is god?" There in Moab, Elimelech died, as did both of his sons. They had left the place they belonged, and they reaped what they sowed. Sam felt a peace flood his soul. By God's grace, he had stayed where God wanted him. Sam remembered the story of Israel crossing the Red Sea. In the middle of God's will, they had trouble, but God made a way through their trial. The difference between them and Elimelech was obedience. Trials would come, but God would make a way for those who obeyed.

Sam was tired. Though it was early, he decided to go to sleep. Glancing at the window, he saw that Hope, the bitterroot flower, was still sitting on the windowsill. How Esther had loved that flower. The thought of Esther brought tears, but a peace came with the tears.

Duke curled up on the rug by the bed and sighed. Sam rubbed his back and the dog rolled over so that Sam could reach his belly. The dog was old but getting along well. Sam was thankful for him.

Soon, Sam laid his head on the pillow and listened as the sounds of night increased. The frogs at the lake were conducting a symphony. The crickets had joined in. Somewhere a lone wolf howled and an owl hooted.

As the sun began to set, it cast shadows on the Silver Arrow. For the first time in months, hope stirred and a peace that passed understanding settled in.

"God makes no mistakes," Sam whispered before he fell asleep.

My Testimony

Psalm 9:1, "I will praise thee, O LORD, with my whole heart; I will shew forth all thy marvellous works."

Again the Lord has blessed. I thank Him for all that He has done. The completion of this book is only one of the many blessings He has bestowed on me.

I want to thank all those that read the first book the Lord helped me write, Jew Hiders. Your kind words and interest were such an encouragement to me. I know many people prayed for me, and I count that a great blessing.

I have always enjoyed reading and writing. When my family would go to watch a high school basketball game, I would bring books to read. The Lord must have been preparing me for the time when He would use me to write.

One of the things that really encouraged me to write is the testimony of my Grandma McBride. One day, I asked her to tell me about when she trusted Christ as her Saviour. Grandma told me that when she was young she was reading an Elsie Dinsmore book, and the girl in the book gave her heart to Jesus. Right there, my Grandma asked the Lord to save her because of the testimony in that book. My prayer for these books is that someone will get saved because of reading them. My friend, if you have never seen yourself as a sinner and have never put your trust in Christ alone to save you from your sin, then you are missing out on the greatest blessing you could ever have.

I was saved at the age of six and a half. I don't regret it at all. There's nothing like knowing you are saved and on your way to Heaven. If you're not saved I beg you to accept Christ as your personal Lord and Saviour. The Bible says in Acts 2:21, "And it shall come to pass, that whosoever shall call on the name of the Lord shall be saved."

Whosoever means anyone. There are some that teach that God picks and chooses those whom He will and will not save, but that is a lie. This verse says, "Whosoever".

If you won't get saved, then your life will be a mess. Twice in the book of Isaiah, we are told that there is no peace for the wicked. Isaiah 48:22, "There is no peace, saith the LORD, unto the wicked." Isaiah 57:21, "There is no peace, saith my God, to the wicked."

Then after you die, you will go to a place called hell. In this day and age, people make light of hell. Some people say hell does not exist, but God said there is a hell. The Bible says in Psalms 9:17, "The wicked shall be turned into hell, and all the nations that forget God."

You may say, "Well, that verse says, 'The wicked shall be turned into hell.' I'm really not that bad."

The Bible says in Romans 3:10, "As it is written, There is none righteous, no, not one:"

Everyone is wicked in the sight of God, but if we will put our trust in the shed blood of Jesus Christ, we can be forgiven and made acceptable.

Ephesians 1:6 says, "To the praise of the glory of his grace, wherein he hath made us accepted in the beloved."

Won't you please ask Jesus to save you? Then you too can know real peace and joy.